I0625143

LADY *of the* TWO LANDS

ELIZABETH DELISI

Tirgearr Publishing

Published by Tirgearr Publishing
Ireland
www.tirgearrpublishing.com

ISBN 978-1-910234-27-3

A CIP catalogue record for this book is
available from the British Library.

10 9 8 7 6 5 4 3 2 1

DEDICATION

To my parents, who told me I could be anything I wanted

To my dear friend Lynne...I miss you every day

And to Dan, my hero in this or any century

ACKNOWLEDGEMENTS

My deepest gratitude goes out to several people who were helpful in the writing of this book:

Edward F. Wente, Professor of Egyptology, Emeritus, University of Chicago, directed me to several scholarly articles about ancient Egyptian coronation ceremonies.

Marie Parsons, author of "Deir el-Bahri" and several other articles at the Tour Egypt website, assisted me with the route to Hatshepsut's temple at Deir el-Bahri.

And Eloise Jarvis McGraw's novel, Mara, Daughter of the Nile, launched me on a lifelong love of all things Egyptian.

My critique partners, Vonda, Kim, and Margery, were tireless in their efforts to help me clean up my prose; and Maureen assisted me with many frantic Internet searches, looking for pictures of Egyptian crowns or temples or boats.

Lastly, my husband Dan was my first and most important reader, providing abundant feedback, thoughtful suggestions, and constant encouragement. I couldn't have finished the book without him.

CHAPTER 1

There it was again—that prickling, crawly sensation, as though someone had run a velvety feather up the back of her neck, causing all the delicate hairs to stand on end. Harriet Williams snapped her head around, sure someone must be watching her *this* time. But, as always, the room was empty. Sighing, she brushed away the damp tendrils of wavy brown hair clinging to her forehead with the back of her hand.

The stone floor of the museum was uncomfortable for prolonged sitting, but it was the only way to stay relatively cool in the warm, musty Egyptian exhibit room. She straightened her shoulders and rotated them a few times, stretched to get the kinks out of her back. She'd only imagined someone was watching her—what other explanation could there be? The museum was closed for the night, and she was alone. Hattie bent again over her sketchpad.

The scene of Hatshepsut being crowned ruler of Egypt took shape under the deft strokes of her charcoal pencil. She had Amun's temple at Karnak in place, crowds of priests and courtiers looking on while the High Priest of Amun placed the double crown on the head of the first woman to rule ancient Egypt as pharaoh.

The fragments of tomb paintings, gilded throne, and scepters in the glass case provided for her a feeling of authenticity that she captured in the sketch. But the face—Hatshepsut's face—refused to come to life. She couldn't get a feel for her features, and they remained flat and lifeless on the page.

Something tickled her ear, like the warm breath of a whispering lover. Hattie jerked away from the touch and leapt to her feet.

1

What in heaven's name was going on? Her imagination was working overtime…but not on the problem of how to render Hatshepsut's features in the illustration. Instead, she found herself conjuring up visions of evildoers lurking in shadowy doorways.

Disgusted, she gathered up her pencils and pad and left the room through a small door in the rear marked "No Admittance—Staff Only".

She wound her way down a dimly lit corridor, past closed wooden doors with names painted on them in black. The last door, marked "Thomas Harris, Egyptian Curator", was still open, the overhead fluorescent light burning.

"Tom," she said, bursting into the office, "I can't get her face right." She slumped down onto a chair in front of a battered wooden desk.

A heavyset, middle-aged man with graying hair and kindly features looked up from the papers spread across the desk and smiled gently. "Calm down, Hattie. We have plenty of time before the manuscript's due. When I asked you to do the illustrations for my book, I didn't mean for you to get all worked up. I thought you'd enjoy it, and I knew you could use the work." He raised his eyebrows. "So, what's the problem?"

She sighed and ran her fingers through her hair. "I don't know. I can't seem to make Hatshepsut's face come alive. Her statues are so stylized, I can't imagine what she really looked like—the woman, not the queen. Here, see for yourself." She thrust her sketchpad under his nose.

He took it from her and studied the drawing. "This is really wonderful, Hattie," he said after a minute. "You've captured the spirit of the proceedings perfectly, all the ceremony and splendor, the ritual, the crowds—just as I knew you would. But I see what you mean about Hatshepsut." He frowned. "I don't know how much more help I can give you. The statues you've seen are the only images of her in the museum. We don't know if they really resemble her or not. But if they're accurate, I'd say she looked a lot like you. Your skin is probably a bit fairer, your hair lighter, but you have her expressive eyes and her slender figure."

2

"You think Hatshepsut looked like me?" Hattie shook her head. "You must be imagining things, too. She was a queen—a pharaoh! I'm sure she looked nothing like plain-Jane me. Nothing at all."

Tom chuckled. "You're much too hard on yourself. You're a very attractive woman."

Hattie snorted.

"Well," he said with mock severity, "I did lend you several books on Egypt, with additional information about Hatshepsut. Have you read even one of them yet?"

"No. I've only flipped through them," she mumbled. "I should've known you'd scold me about that! But I do have other commissions in progress, you know. Besides," she added defensively, "ancient history is boring. I have absolutely nothing in common with a woman who lived thirty-five hundred years ago."

"I'll bet you have more in common with her than you think," Tom said. "She was a woman, like you. She had a life, friends, family, a job—like you. She had favorite foods, probably enjoyed music and art, had some hobbies."

"Maybe." Hattie was unconvinced. Surely a queen had a large family and many friends; she had people who depended on her, people who loved her. Hattie had no family left, few friends, and not even a cat to come home to at night. Her career *was* her life.

Tom sighed. "So, what's this about imagining things?"

"Oh, don't worry about it." She waved her hand. "I imagined someone was watching me. Naturally, no one was there, no matter how quickly I turned around. I've been at it too long, I guess. Or maybe I've seen *The Mummy* one too many times."

He laughed and handed back the sketchbook. "What are you going to do about Hatshepsut's face?"

"I'm not sure. Maybe a good night's sleep will give me more perspective." She yawned hugely and stretched out her arms. "I don't have any other ideas right now. I'm too tired to think straight."

Tom steepled his index fingers together and tapped them thoughtfully against his lips. "I have a suggestion. We have a necklace in our collection that's reputed to have belonged to Hatshepsut. It isn't being displayed currently, but I'd be glad to show it to you. Maybe it would help you to put a human face on a legend. What do you say?"

"Why not? It might do the trick."

Hattie followed Tom down another dimly lit corridor to a room marked "Egyptian Artifacts". He opened the door and turned on the overhead light, then ushered her in.

She glanced around in dismay. The room looked like an oversized closet—windowless, dusty, and cluttered with storage cabinets. It was enough to make anyone claustrophobic. Tom strode to one of the cabinets, opened a drawer, and removed a large, flat box. He placed the box gently on a small table and removed the lid.

Hattie gasped and her breath caught in her throat. Nestled in a protective bed of acid-free paper, a pectoral necklace glittered and sparkled in the muted light of the lone overhead bulb. Row upon row of turquoise, lapis lazuli, gold and colored glass beads formed the outspread wings for the central figure of a falcon, fashioned entirely of gold with inset eyes of green jasper. Inscribed hieroglyphics covered the body of the bird. Delicate golden links held the broad, flexible collar together.

"Oh, Tom," she whispered. "It's the most beautiful thing I've ever seen!"

Tom grinned. "I thought you'd like it. Do you think it'll help?"

"Yes. Definitely!" she said, her fatigue evaporating like mist in the morning sun. "Can I bring it out to the exhibit room?"

"I'd rather you didn't," he said. "Even though the museum's closed, I think it's safer if it remains here in this room. Out there, I'd have to lock it away in a display case." He spread his hands apologetically. "Can you work here? I know it's a little crowded."

"Of course." Hattie nodded emphatically. "I understand. Just give me an hour, and I should be finished."

Tom glanced at his watch. "I can't wait that long. I've got to go. I have a dinner meeting with the museum board of directors in forty-five minutes." He paused. "I'll tell you what. I'll lock the employee entrance on my way out. The museum closed fifteen minutes ago, and all the other doors are locked. You can take as long as you like, but put the necklace back in the cabinet when you're through, and make sure the employee door locks behind you when you leave. And don't forget to turn out the lights," he added, winking.

"Perfect! Will do, boss." Hattie saluted smartly.

Tom laughed, then left her alone. As soon as his footsteps died away, she flipped open her sketch pad to a clean page and set it on the table next to the necklace. Before she tried again to imagine Hatshepsut's features, she wanted to make a detailed drawing of the collar.

Within half an hour, she had the broad outlines of the necklace faithfully reproduced on the paper. Yawning, she laid her pencil beside the tablet. Even the beauty of the necklace couldn't keep her awake forever. Maybe it was time to call it a day. She could duplicate the intricate hieroglyphs tomorrow.

No sooner had she decided to quit than the back of her neck prickled, and a warm breeze stroked her cheek. Not again! She whipped around, determined to catch the furtive watcher this time. Her left arm hit the partially open door, which promptly slammed shut.

Hattie reached for the doorknob and turned it, giving the door a jerk. It remained firmly closed. She jiggled the knob and pulled on it, but it was quite obviously locked. "Great!" she muttered. "Just what I need. I wonder how long that meeting of Tom's will last?"

Her mouth dropped open as a horrible thought occurred to her. What if Tom didn't return after the meeting? What if he went straight home? "Tomorrow's Sunday," she reminded herself grimly. "I might be stuck here in this…this broom closet for two days!" There was no one at her apartment to miss her or report her absence—not even a dog to bark and alert the neighbors.

Hattie banged on the door. "Is anyone there? Let me out!" She shouted and beat on the door with her palms, but all was ominously silent. If someone *had* been watching her, they had no intention of helping her out of her dilemma.

At last, resigned to her fate, she returned to her sketchpad. "If I'm going to be stuck in here, I might as well finish my work," she murmured. "Tom's bound to come back—I'm sure he will." Her voice echoed unconvincingly in the dusty, claustrophobic room.

Picking up her pencil, she focused deliberately on copying the tiny hieroglyphics with extreme precision. Gradually, she became absorbed in her work and forgot her predicament. Minutes flowed by with the only sound in the room the scratching of her pencil on the paper.

At last, she completed the final symbol on her detailed drawing and set down her pencil with a twinge of disappointment. She was curiously drawn to the glittering possession of the ancient, yet strangely modern woman. Hatshepsut had ruled Egypt fifteen hundred years before Christ, at a time when women were considered no more important than servants or dogs. How had she managed it?

The vagrant breeze whispered past her face again, leaving a whiff of exquisite perfume in its wake. A rustle, like the caress of costly linen against bare skin, drew her attention. She felt a strong presence, though she knew she was alone in the tiny room.

"Touch it."

The words were so faint, Hattie wasn't sure she'd actually heard them.

"Who's there?" she asked, though she didn't expect to get a response. The room was too small to hide anyone.

"Touch the necklace."

Hattie spun around, searching for the source of the barely audible words. "Tom, is that you? If it's you, I don't think this is funny! Open the door right now." She thumped it with her fist for emphasis.

There was no response.

Hattie turned back to the exquisitely fashioned falcon. Maybe it was her overworked imagination playing a trick on her, but the advice seemed sound. Perhaps if she touched the necklace, she could make a connection—psychic, empathic?— with the long-dead monarch. The necklace was strangely compelling, like a long forgotten yet treasured memory.

She reached out slowly, cautiously. As her fingertips gently grazed the golden bird, an electric shock pulsed through her and a sudden wave of dizziness sapped her strength.

"Come to me," the ghostly voice whispered, stronger now. "Come to me. I have need of you."

The sweet, cloying scent of incense filled Hattie's nostrils, and flashes of light exploded behind her eyes. Her vision blurred; she felt as if she were reeling, falling down a long, dark tunnel. Gasping, she reached out blindly for something, anything, to steady herself. Her fingers skimmed across the surface of the table and fastened around the necklace. Clutching it, she fell heavily to the floor as everything went black.

* * *

Hattie opened her eyes, but she saw nothing. Everything was still as black as midnight. Her heart leapt to her throat. Was she blind? Had someone overpowered her and locked her in a dark, eerie cell?

Suddenly, a cooling breath of comfort filtered through her and she relaxed, sighing. She felt the ghostly presence again, but she was no longer afraid. She turned and saw, glowing like a lamp in the darkness, a lovely, slender woman wearing a diaphanous white gown and an array of glittering jewels. Her reddish-gold hair was braided intricately, and her slim feet were encased in delicate sandals. She looked like Hattie, and yet she didn't. She exuded an aura of graciousness, elegance—and antiquity. It was as though Hattie stared at the portrait of a long-dead ancestor.

"Who…who are you?" Hattie whispered. "Do I know you?"

"Yes—and no," the woman responded.

It was the same voice she'd heard in the storage room of the museum. Hattie was sure of it. She felt the woman's words in her head more than she heard them with her ears. "What do you mean, yes and no?" she asked.

"I am your past, and your future."

"I have no idea what you're talking about." Hattie shook her head. "Where am I? Why am I here? Did you bring me here?"

"I have searched for you for millennia," the mysterious woman responded. "I have waited many ages for the one who could fulfill my destiny and my life, which was unjustly cut short so long ago."

Hattie shuddered. This woman was definitely out to lunch. "Listen, I don't know who you are or what you want, but I suggest you let me go at once. Tom will be looking for me, you know."

The woman shrugged slightly as the glow around her diminished and brightened, like a star twinkling in the dark night sky. "I am sorry, but I have need of you. The thread of my life was severed before its time, and you must finish what I started."

Hattie tried to edge away. Hadn't she read somewhere it was important not to challenge the delusions of a crazy person? "Why me? I have a life of my own. I don't want to fulfill your destiny." As an afterthought, she added, "I'm sorry."

"Ah…but my destiny is your destiny. You are fated to perform the task stolen from me. Only then can you resume your own life."

"And what is that task?" Hattie asked suspiciously. "Do you want me to bring you the broomstick of the Wicked Witch of the West?"

The woman laughed, a sparkling sound like water splashing in a fountain. "Some have called me witch, but none could truthfully claim I was wicked. Nay, the task you must fulfill is to protect the heir to the throne, my stepson, Prince Tuthmosis. You must determine the identity of the betrayer who cut short my life and who also threatens the young prince. I was close to discovering the name of the traitor, but he learned I was a danger to him and had me killed." She smiled grimly. "I knew the necklace would bring you to me. Now, you must find him. Only then can I resume the path of my life as the gods intended, and you can return to yours."

"Tuthmosis? Traitors?" Hattie backed up another step, giving up all hope of going along with the crazy woman. The conversation was so ridiculous, it was difficult to participate in. "Even if what you say is true, why me? Why am I the one who has to go back and solve your problems?"

"Because you are of my blood. You sprang from my stock. Though the link is distant, my blood runs truer in your veins than in any who came before you." The woman stepped closer. "Only you can right this grave injustice. You must protect Tuthmosis. He is but a boy, and without me to protect him, he is helpless."

"Now you're saying I'm Egyptian? You must be crazy! I'm as American as they come. Just who are you anyway?"

"I am King's Great Wife, God's Wife of Amun, Lady of the Two Lands—Hatshepsut." Hatshepsut reached out and touched Hattie's cheek with a feather-light touch, but Hattie felt it in every fiber of her being, like an electric shock.

A gasp died in Hattie's throat. Her head swam, her heart pounded; blackness rushed up to engulf her, and she surrendered to a force she didn't understand and couldn't overcome.

CHAPTER 2

Hattie awoke with regret. Her head pounded fiercely, the potent scent of incense still lingering in her nostrils. She groaned, but hesitated to open her eyes. She didn't know if the crazy woman was still there—and if she were, what she might do to Hattie next.

"Amun be praised! She lives!" A heartfelt, deep male voice broke the stillness of the room. "Are you all right, Majesty? Do you know your name?"

"H…Hattie," she croaked, her eyes still squeezed tightly shut. The deep voice sounded nothing like the ghostly woman who'd claimed to be Hatshepsut.

"Open your eyes and let me gaze into them, I pray you," the voice commanded.

Hattie opened one eye slowly, then the other. A breathtakingly handsome man bent over her, his long, dark hair hanging down around his face. Concern etched lines across his broad forehead and from his aquiline nose down to his sensual lips. Deep brown eyes widened in puzzlement as Hattie's gaze met his. "Majesty! Do you not know me?"

Her thoughts swam in futile circles. What had happened to her? Where was she? Who was this man? She was sure he wasn't on the museum staff, and he didn't have the efficient manner of a paramedic. Shouldn't he be asking her the name of the President, or the day of the month? Had he called her "Majesty"? What did that mean?

She glanced over his shoulder and around the room. Whitewashed walls, covered with vividly-painted scenes of stylized ancient Egyptian figures spearing fish, baking bread, and making offerings to the gods, rose up to meet a midnight blue ceiling, dotted with stars. Good, she was still in the museum—somewhere in the Egyptian wing, though she didn't recognize it immediately. The crazy woman must have run away when Hattie fainted.

She turned her attention to her companion. "Nay, I do not know you. Were you the one who found me in the storage room? If so, I thank you."

The man frowned. "Majesty, I caught you in my arms when you swooned at the funerary rites for your husband, the Great God, may he live forever. I feared you were dead, your *ka* flown to the gods. Thank Amun I was wrong. I know nothing of a storage room. Such rooms are visited only by servants."

Hattie stared up at the man bending over her. He appeared to be entirely sincere, but she couldn't make sense of anything he said. What husband? What funeral? Servants? She struggled to push herself upright for a better look at her surroundings, but she was still weak and her head swam dizzily. Instantly, his strong arm encircled her shoulders and he gently helped her to a sitting position.

Her eyes widened as she looked around the small room again. Colorful figures marched across the rough walls and floor, and stars gleamed from the ceiling. Two small, high-set windows in one wall let in streams of sunlight and sparkling dust motes, while several tightly woven baskets of various sizes lined the opposite wall. A curtained door in one wall and an uncurtained door in another appeared to be the only exits.

She lay on a low, uncomfortable bed, covered with a scratchy linen sheet. She saw no other furniture in the room, save the wooden stool on which her companion sat. Absolutely nothing looked familiar. "Where am I?" she cried, forcing down the panic that threatened to rise in her throat. "Am I in the museum? Where have you taken me?"

"You are in your own bed chamber, Majesty," the man said soothingly. "You have had a great shock today. Please lie down." He gently pressed her back into a reclining position.

Confused, she decided she must have hit her head harder than she thought when she fainted and fell in the storage room. That would explain the strange woman as well—she was nothing more than a hallucination. Tom would certainly get a piece of her mind the next time she saw him. He had some nerve, leaving the door locked with her sitting inside! *At least I haven't broken any bones,* she thought, passing a shaking hand across her face.

Suddenly, Hattie jerked her hand away as if it had stung her. Staring at it, she felt the blood drain from her cheeks. It wasn't her hand. It was attached to her arm, moved when she willed it, but it didn't look like her own ink-stained hand with practical, short fingernails. It was a little smaller, golden-brown, with slender fingers and elegant, oval nails. Horrified, she threw back the sheet that covered her. A brief moment of dismay at discovering she was totally nude gave way to panic when she saw that the slim, sun-browned body lying on the bed looked nothing like her own pale, freckled frame. She reached up to her head and pulled a long lock of hair down in front of her eyes. It was wavy, like hers, but much longer and, instead of chestnut brown, it was a rich red-gold color.

"What has happened to me?" she cried, her voice breaking. "I demand that you tell me, right now!"

Her companion pulled the sheet up under her chin and said in a low, comforting voice, "Everything is all right, Majesty. You have suffered a great loss. You need to sleep." He lifted an alabaster goblet to her lips. "Drink," he urged.

Obediently, she sipped. The liquid in the cup tasted strong, sweet and alcoholic. She sank back onto the bed. Her head buzzed and the pictures on the walls swam into indistinct blurs. What had he put in the wine? Had he drugged her? She fought to keep her eyes open.

"Sleep, Majesty," the man whispered.

With his warm hand gently stroking her hair, Hattie stopped struggling and dropped off into unconsciousness.

* * *

"Fool! Are you incapable of performing even the smallest task?" The stocky, shaven-headed priest strode back and forth in front of a cringing guard kneeling on the floor, head bowed.

"I am sorry, holy one," the guard whispered, glancing up. "I did as you instructed. Amun help me, I put the poison into her cup. I saw her drink it, I swear by Amun! I know not why she still lives."

"Well, something went wrong because she is not dead. Did you spill any of the poison? She fell to the floor in a swoon but did not die. Mayhap the poison was not at full potency." The priest's gaze bored into the hapless guard's eyes.

"Nay, holy one, I did not spill any. I swear by the sacred name of Isis!" He bowed his head again, trembling violently. "She must have a charm or amulet, something to protect her. I know not what."

"*Ast!* Go, then…go. I have no further use for you at this moment. But I warn you—speak of this to no one, or I will personally feed you to the crocodiles." He flapped his hand at the guard.

The guard rose and bowed deeply, then scurried from the room as if the devils of Set the Devourer were after him.

"I can see I must be more careful," the priest muttered. "I must take this task to myself. Lesser ones cannot be trusted. The next time, I shall not fail."

CHAPTER 3

Hattie awoke from a pleasant dream of lying in a man's comforting embrace. She didn't know who the man was, but in her dream, his presence made her feel safe and protected. She was loathe to return to reality.

At last, she opened her eyes. White stars on a blue painted ceiling swam into view. She groaned. Maybe she had a concussion, and was hallucinating. Hospital rooms didn't have painted ceilings, and surely she would have been taken to a hospital by now—if anyone had found her. Was she still lying unconscious on the storage room floor and this was a dream? Or was she in the hospital, and all this a painkiller-induced hallucination—the crazy woman, the painted chamber, the body that wasn't her own, the gorgeous man?

Her gaze wandered around the room, coming to rest on her ever-present male companion seated across from her. Already, he seemed her only friend in a strange land. Was he a doctor, or was he a figment of her imagination?

Noticing her eyes open, he rose and strode to her side. "How do you feel, Majesty?"

"Better, I think," she said tentatively. Her voice sounded odd to her, higher and lighter than usual. Weak from shock, probably. "I am thirsty. May I have something to drink?"

"Of course, Majesty. Right away." He walked to the doorway and clapped his hands. "Nesi!"

At once, the curtain over the door was pushed aside and a dark-haired young woman stepped into the room. She wore a long white dress, but she was most definitely not a nurse—her dress was draped to expose one small, tanned breast. "Aye, Lord?" she said, bowing her head.

"Bring bread, dates, and wine for Her Majesty."

"Aye, Lord." Nesi left the room as quickly as she had entered.

Hattie shook her head, trying to clear it, but succeeded only in making it pound. Something strange had happened to her, and she couldn't make sense of it. The young woman called Nesi was not the only one dressed in an odd fashion; she herself lay naked under the coarse sheet, with no recollection of anyone undressing her. *Which is probably just as well*, she mused.

Her companion's clothing was strange also, though not unpleasant. He wore a pleated white kilt fastened low on his lean hips. He was shirtless; his bronzed chest bare and smooth. A wide collar of gold and golden armbands accented his broad shoulders, muscular arms and torso. Definitely not a doctor's garb!

His speech sounded odd, archaic. She couldn't put her finger on just what was different, though. Did he have an unusual accent, or an old-fashioned vocabulary? If only her blasted headache would go away, perhaps she could figure it out...

Comprehension slowly dawned. He wasn't speaking English. It wasn't French. It wasn't Spanish. It was no language she had ever heard spoken. But if that were true, how could she understand him? How could he understand her? For, as strange as it seemed, she appeared to be speaking the unknown language as well. If this was a dream, it was the most bizarre one she'd ever had. She had no idea her subconscious was so inventive.

"I am confused," she whispered, massaging her temples with both hands. "I do not...I do not remember what happened to me. Can you tell me?"

The man pulled up his stool next to her bed and sat. "You have not been yourself since your husband, the Great God, died," he said, sympathy warming his voice. "You have not eaten or slept in days. You are distraught. I will assist you in any way I can, Majesty."

Hattie smiled, her bottom lip trembling. "Thank you. Mayhap, with your help, I will remember what..." She shook her head, then winced at the pain throbbing behind her eyes. "Where am I?"

"In your bedchamber, Majesty. Have I not told you this?"

"But this is not my...oh, never mind. Where is my bedchamber? I mean," she added hastily, "in what city is this house?"

The man smiled. "That question I can answer easily, Majesty. You are in your royal palace in the city of Thebes."

Thebes. Hattie was no scholar, but even she knew Thebes was in Egypt. Was this man crazy—or was she? Was someone playing a nasty practical joke on her? If it were Tom, she'd never forgive him. First, the mysterious woman who claimed to be Hatshepsut, and now this.

"Where is Tom?" she demanded. "Tell him I want to see him at once. This has gone on long enough. Tell him I do not find this humorous."

"Tom?" The man's voice sounded puzzled. "I regret that I do not know anyone called Tom. Who is he—a servant of the Great God's, mayhap? It is not the name of a nobleman, of that I am certain."

Nesi returned to the room at that moment, bearing a tray of round, flat bread loaves and dates, and a flagon that Hattie supposed held wine. She placed the items on a lidded basket beside Hattie's bed and silently backed out of the room, bowing.

"Bread, Majesty?" The man tore off a large piece from one of the loaves and held it out to her.

"In a minute." She tried another avenue of investigation. "Why do you keep calling me Majesty? Why do you not use my name?"

The man's strong brown fingers toyed with the chunk of bread. "It would not be seemly for me to use your name, Majesty."

"But you do know my name?" she persisted.

"Of course, Majesty. You are Hatshepsut, King's Great Wife and God's Wife of Amun."

Hatshepsut? Now, she *knew* she was dreaming. The illustration she had been drawing of Hatshepsut's coronation and the sight of her glittering necklace must have been on her mind when she passed out—that was why she dreamed she'd spoken to Hatshepsut, and why this man called her by that name.

A great wave of relief swept over her, leaving her limp in its wake. Sooner or later, she'd rouse from this bizarre dream. In the meantime, she might as well play along and enjoy herself. What could it hurt? At the very least, she'd have a fascinating story to tell Tom when it was all over. After she was through chewing him out, of course.

"I see. Of course. Well, I would prefer that you call me Hattie. Majesty is too formal. I care not for it," she said, in what she hoped was an imperial tone.

"I dare not presume, Majesty," the man protested.

"Presume. I command you." She struggled to hold back a smile.

"Very well, Majes—Hattie." The man stumbled over the unfamiliar name. "In truth, I have not heard you called thus since your childhood."

"My childhood?" Incredible! But then, it made a perverse sort of sense—Hatshepsut, Hattie. How convenient! She was rather pleased with the inventiveness of her subconscious. "Tell me about the funeral rites for…for my husband," she urged.

"Ah, Majes—Hattie, a glorious sight indeed! Priests of Amun escorted the Great God in all his splendor on his journey across the Nile and to the Necropolis. They performed the necessary rites and spells to insure His Majesty life eternal. Once in the tomb, the High Priest performed the Opening of the Mouth." The man paused and cleared his throat. "At that moment you cried aloud and collapsed, and I fear I can tell you no more. I caught you in my arms and returned you across the river—here to the palace—certain you had died of grief."

"Died. Aye, you said that. But I am not dead."

"Nay, you are not, and I confess I do not understand. I waited with the body for the…waited with you until Hapuseneb, High Priest of Amun, could come to take you to the Necropolis, but something detained him. Just as I was about to send for him again, you awoke. Amun be praised," he added quickly.

Hattie's heart beat faster and her pulse raced. The details of the funeral rites were unfamiliar, yet they sounded plausible. And Hatshepsut's titles were a mystery to her—she had only heard her referred to as pharaoh—yet she had heard them twice now, once from the crazy woman and once from this man. If this was indeed only a dream or a phantom of her subconscious mind, how could she suddenly know details and historical facts she had never read or learned? Was she inventing things that only sounded correct? Or were they actually facts buried in her subconscious?

If it were a dream, it was the most vivid one she'd ever experienced. She saw light glinting off the gold around the man's neck and biceps; she smelled the sharp, sweet scent of the wine. She pinched herself, hard, and her arm stung fiercely. Was it possible to feel pain in a dream, in a phantom body? What if this was all real? What if it wasn't a dream or a hallucination, but somehow she had truly been transported back through time to land in Hatshepsut's court?

Even if she had been transported back in time, who was she? She wasn't Hatshepsut, so why would this man and the servant believe she was? She was Hattie Williams, from Chicago. Yet she didn't *look* like herself. Did she look like Queen Hatshepsut? And if so, why? Hattie groaned. She had many more questions than answers—and she wasn't altogether sure she wanted to know those answers.

Her companion had said he feared Hatshepsut had died during her husband's funeral. He had seemed genuinely shocked when she opened her eyes. Was that the key? Had Hatshepsut actually died during her husband's funeral? Had Hattie somehow taken her place? But that didn't make sense. The real queen had lived to rule as pharaoh. Hadn't she? What was it the crazy ghost had said—that her life and destiny had been cut short? But that didn't agree with the small amount of Egyptian history Hattie knew.

"One more question, Mister…" Hattie frowned. What was his name? Had he told her? "I am sorry, but I fear I have forgotten who you are." She gestured at her aching head. "I am not myself. Will you forgive me?"

"I would not presume to judge you, and there is nothing to forgive, for you have been gravely ill. I am Royal Tutor to your daughter, Princess Neferure."

A daughter. The plot had become ever more twisted and tangled. Hattie sighed, massaging her temples again. "Of course, you are my daughter's tutor…but what is your name?"

"My name is Senemut, Hattie. Do you not remember me?" He seemed distressed, though her previous lapses of memory had not appeared to bother him.

Hattie's mouth dropped open, and a flush burned her cheeks. Oh, yes, she knew him now. Not from personal acquaintance, but from what little she *had* learned of Hatshepsut's life. Her stomach lurched as she realized this was not a nightmare produced by her subconscious. This was real! She didn't understand how it had happened, or why, but somehow, in some fashion, she had been transported into the past, into the life and the body of Hatshepsut.

Senemut's name had made it frighteningly clear: the handsome man bending over her, the man who had been her constant companion and only comfort throughout this inexplicable nightmare, was royal architect and constant companion to the Pharaoh Hatshepsut—and, quite probably, her lover.

CHAPTER 4

"Majesty? Hattie? Are you all right? By Amun, I must send for the royal physician…"

The concern in Senemut's voice shook Hattie out of her trance. "Nay, nay, there is no need for that. Of course I know you." She tried to smile, though she feared it was more of a grimace. "The past few days have been difficult."

"How thoughtless of me! You must rest." He rose from the stool and walked across the room, then slowly turned and came back to her side. "There is one thing I must ask. Will Your Majesty see the princess now? She has been most distraught during your illness."

Hattie didn't know how old Hatshepsut's daughter was, but the child would surely recognize an imposter—even if the imposter looked exactly like her mother. She needed some time to pull herself together, to figure out what to do. She shook her head. "I fear I am not up to it yet, Senemut. Tell her, please, that I will speak with her as soon as—"

She broke off as the curtain flew aside and a small form burst into the room. A beautiful child of about three, with dark hair and eyes and golden skin, flung herself onto Hattie's recumbent form, knocking the breath out of her.

"Mother!" she cried, throwing her arms around Hattie's neck. "Aneksi would not let me come to see you. So I ran away from her."

Hattie frowned at Senemut over Neferure's head as she tried to catch her breath.

"Aneksi is the child's nurse," he murmured.

Ah, of course, the nanny. Hattie stroked the small head.

"There, there," she said awkwardly, as soon as she could speak. "Everything is all right now."

"But Aneksi told me you were dead! Both you and my royal father." The child raised her head to stare at Hattie with wide eyes, a tear quivering on her round, pudgy cheek.

"Well, as you can see, I am perfectly healthy. So Aneksi was wrong, and you have nothing to fear." Hattie had little experience with children and wasn't sure just what to say, but she kept her voice soothing and gentle.

"Is my royal father alive, too? Is he coming back?" Hope blazed across the small face.

An icy hand clenched Hattie's heart. "Nay, little one, he is not," she whispered. "I am sorry."

Neferure dissolved into tears and flung herself again onto Hattie's chest. Hattie put her arms around the child and patted her back until the storm subsided.

At last, the girl raised her head, swiped her cheeks with her palms and hiccupped.

"Better?" Hattie asked, stroking the tear-stained cheek.

Neferure nodded. "Will I have to marry my brother Tuthmosis now that my royal father is dead? I do not want to marry him. I do not like him. He puts frogs in my bed and pulls my hair."

"Marry your brother? I should say not. Why, I have never heard of such a preposterous..." She faltered to a stop. Over the child's head, Senemut frowned, clearly puzzled. She needed to watch herself; she didn't want to put her foot in her mouth and say something totally out of character. The sum of her knowledge of Egyptian customs and traditions would fill a thimble. "You need not worry about that now. You are not old enough to think of marriage yet. We will discuss it later."

Neferure grinned and stuck out her tongue at Senemut.

"Time to return to Aneksi, little one," Senemut said, taking her hand. "She must be very worried about you. You were naughty to run away."

Neferure pouted. "I want to stay here with Mother."

"Your mother needs to rest," Senemut said in a firm tone.

"Out, now."

Neferure flounced across the room, then turned back for an instant. "Mother, you look different."

"Of course, she looks different," Senemut said before Hattie could respond. "She has been ill. Hurry, now." The child made a face at her tutor before disappearing swiftly from the room.

Senemut chuckled. "The little one has spirit."

Spirit and intelligence, Hattie thought. How long could she fool the child into thinking she was her mother?

"I fear you have given the princess false hope," Senemut continued. "She must indeed marry her brother, your stepson. How else can he secure his claim to the throne, since he is the son of a lesser wife?"

Stepson? How many other relatives lurked within the palace walls, ready to expose her at the slightest misstep? "Surely, she is too young to marry anyone at this time," Hattie said. "She is but a baby. I will hear no more of it."

"Very well," Senemut said, confusion marked across the strong planes of his face. "I will take my leave now and allow you to rest."

Impulsively, Hattie held out her hand to him. "Thank you, Senemut, for all your help. I am most grateful."

Senemut hesitated, then took her hand in both of his, lowered his head and kissed it gently. "Sleep well, Majesty," he said, and strode from the room.

Hot sparks shot up her arm from the spot his lips had touched. She put her hand to her suddenly flushed cheek. What had she gotten herself into?

* * *

"Bring me wine, Hori!" Senemut shouted to a bald, wizened servant as he paced the floor in his palace apartments.

"Aye, Lord." Hori bowed deeply. "May I bring food as well? You appear tired. When was your last meal?"

Senemut glanced at Hori. It was not like him to bow. He and Senemut were on familiar terms and had been so since Senemut's childhood. Perhaps his harsh tone of voice was responsible for the unnecessary display of subservience. He softened his expression and smiled at the old man. "Always, you see to my comfort and you give me sound counsel. You have been more a father to me than my own ever was! I apologize for growling at you, old friend." He rubbed his stomach. "Aye, you are right. It has been overlong since I have eaten. Bring food as well and join me at the meal, if you would. I have something I wish your opinion on."

Hori grinned. "It would be my pleasure. It has been some time since you last sought my advice. I feared you had grown too wise to seek the opinions of your old tutor."

"Nay, I will never be too wise for your counsel, though at times I fear I am too proud. But in this I would hear your thoughts. Go now, and do not tarry."

Before long, Hori returned bearing a tray with dishes of roasted fish, figs and cheese, a round loaf of bread, and a flagon of wine. He set the food before Senemut. "Eat, and tell me your troubles," he said, munching on a fig.

Senemut attacked the food with relish while Hori watched silently. At last Senemut pushed aside the tray with a contented sigh. "I was hungrier than I knew! But now I am content."

"So, tell me what ails you." Hori shifted to a more comfortable position on the low stool.

"It is Her Majesty Hatshepsut," Senemut began slowly, considering his words. "Since her illness, she has changed. She seems like a…like a different person." He spread his arms helplessly. "I know not how to describe it."

"How has she changed?" Hori asked. "Has her appearance altered, or does she behave in a different fashion?"

"She is confused, but that is to be expected after such a grave illness. Her memory appears faulty, but that, too, is understandable." Senemut paused to organize his thoughts. How could he describe a change he felt more than saw? "What concerns me is her unexpected actions and demeanor. This morning, she told little Neferure that she need not marry her brother." He shook his head. "While Hatshepsut has always been a softhearted woman, she understands the necessity of the marriage to secure Tuthmosis's claim to the throne. Why then does she make this promise she cannot keep, which will only break the child's heart?"

Hori whistled softly. "That seems unlike her, indeed. But illness can cause one to reevaluate priorities and choices. Mayhap she has another husband in mind for the girl—mayhap a diplomatic alliance with Phoenicia or Syria?"

Senemut scowled and scratched his head. "I do not think so. She said the girl was too young to marry, nothing more." How could he explain to Hori his uneasiness at Hatshepsut's behavior? He looked around swiftly, then lowered his voice. "Old friend, I speak to you now of things I would disclose to no one else. It could mean my life, were my words to travel beyond the walls of this room."

Hori waved his hand. "You have always had my loyalty and my silence, Lord. You may depend on it. Please, continue."

Senemut nodded, relieved. He knew he could trust Hori. "She seems more decisive than I have known her to be. Hatshepsut was ever gracious but reserved, conversing more freely with her servants than with her advisors. Now she speaks her mind to all in a most commanding fashion. She sounds more like pharaoh than her husband, the Great God, ever did. Is this a common after-effect of illness, think you?"

Hori frowned. "I have never heard of patients acting thus when they are healed. Mayhap you should consult your physician?"

"Nay, I dare not." Senemut shuddered. If he discussed this with his physician, who knew how far the tale would spread? He was willing to risk it with Hori, but with no one else.

"Then all I can advise you to do is wait and watch her. It may be that her illness has produced this metamorphosis. Mayhap when she is fully healed, she will return to her former self." He studied Senemut intently. "But if she remains this way, can you still serve her?"

"Aye. She is my queen and I must obey." He grinned, remembering her spirited defense of the little princess. "I believe I prefer her with her new boldness and audacity." He rose and put a hand on Hori's shoulder. "Thank you for your counsel, old friend. As always, it is sound. I will wait and watch, and see what changes time brings."

CHAPTER 5

Disturbing images broke Hattie's sleep. She found herself sitting on a gilded throne inside a glass case at the museum, alongside a brightly painted wooden mummy case and a host of smaller items. There was no way for her to get out. Suddenly, Tom appeared, leading a group of tourists on a tour of the museum. He paused at the display case and began to speak about Hatshepsut and her reign, pointing to the items in the case. Hattie leaped up and pounded on the glass, calling his name, but he didn't seem to hear her. He finished his lecture and moved on, turning out the lights as he left the room. It was so dark, and she was so alone...

Hattie awoke with a gasp. Sun streamed in through the high-set windows. It seemed late—she must have slept for a full day. Suddenly ravenous, she looked around for the tray of bread and dates. Sure enough, it lay next to her bed, untouched except for the chunk of bread that Senemut had removed. She leaned over, seized a date and popped it into her mouth. The sweet burst of flavor made her throat ache and her eyes water. If she had any doubts before, she knew now it wasn't a dream—she actually was marooned in ancient Egypt. No dream ever delivered such reality of taste, touch, sight and sound.

Somehow, the necklace had brought her here. Were the hieroglyphics a time-travel incantation, and when she finished copying them, the spell was activated? That didn't seem likely, since she was ignorant of the meaning of the symbols and could very well have set some down incorrectly. Was there a substance, like poison, on the necklace? No, that made no sense either, since Tom and no doubt others had handled it with no ill effect. Was it the type or placement or color of the precious stones?

Hattie had plenty of questions, and absolutely no answers. She also had a splitting headache. *Of all the things I've left behind, I miss aspirin most*, she thought wryly. Then her stomach growled. That need, at least, she could satisfy.

She reached for the bread on the tray and tore off a piece. It felt coarse and gritty in her hands. She took a small bite and chewed experimentally. It was like eating sand. Disappointed, she dropped the rest of the bread onto the tray and sighed. Obviously, a croissant would be out of the question in an era where flour was still ground by hand on a large, flat rock.

The wine, however, was quite good. She finished the wine and dates, then dusted off her hands. Now what? She couldn't go cavorting around the palace totally nude, could she? Hatshepsut was a queen, so she must have had clothes, for heaven's sake. Where would they be?

"Are you there, Hatshepsut?" she murmured. "How about telling me where to find your closet?" Then she shook her head. Even though she accepted now that she was stranded in ancient Egypt, she wasn't convinced she'd actually met and conversed with Hatshepsut on her way here. More likely, that was a hallucination as a result of the blow to her head.

Hattie stood up, wrapping the linen sheet carefully around her like a sarong. She felt a little weak, but her headache was fading. She crossed the room to the row of woven baskets and knelt beside them. What did they contain? Not snakes, she hoped. There was nothing she hated more than snakes.

Cautiously, she removed the lid from the first basket. It contained small alabaster pots and jars, a polished bronze mirror, small paintbrushes, and carved wooden and ivory sticks. She presumed they were all makeup or toiletry items.

Hattie gasped when she opened the second basket. It was filled to the brim with the sparkle of gold and gemstones. She was tempted to search for the pectoral necklace she'd been faithfully reproducing when she passed out in the museum storage room—it might be a key to her return to her own time. She reached into the basket, paused, and then regretfully replaced the lid. Her immediate priority was clothing. She would have to search for the necklace later.

She hit the jackpot with the third basket. Piles of snowy, pleated linen lay starched and folded within. Hattie pulled the uppermost article from the pile and held it up to her with one hand. The linen was so sheer, she could see the faint outline of her hand through it—an amazing feat, considering it must have been hand-woven. But it did seem to be rather scandalously low-cut, along the lines of Nesi's gown.

At that moment, the curtain flew aside and Senemut entered without ceremony. Hattie stood and dropped the gown guiltily. "I was looking for something to wear," she stammered, clutching the sheet more tightly around her.

"Ah, you are recovered! I am pleased to see it," he said. "Would you like me to send for some food, or your servants to bathe and dress you?"

Servants? Would they be male or female-or both? Hattie gulped. She hadn't needed help bathing since she was three, but what would Hatshepsut have done? "Just Nesi, please."

"As you wish, Majesty. Nesi will attend you. When you are ready, she will lead you to the throne room."

"The throne room? Why?"

Senemut looked puzzled. "You are Regent now. Today, you and young Tuthmosis must hear the case brought by Merisu the potter against Ahmose the soldier, and render judgment."

"A case?" Visions of Perry Mason in a courtroom swirled through her mind. "I know not how to handle a case. What must I do?"

"Listen, Majesty. Listen and judge. Amun will guide your heart to the truth."

"I hope so," Hattie murmured. "Very well. Shall I see you there?"

Senemut shook his head. "I must return to my duties as tutor. I have neglected them for far too long." He flashed her a smile, then bowed and left the room.

After a moment, Nesi stepped in. "Majesty," she said, bowing. Hattie smiled at her but made no move. A bewildered frown creasing her brow, Nesi gestured in the direction of the doorway with no curtain. Hattie nodded and preceded her into the room.

A large, sloping stone slab occupied the middle of the floor. There was a small hole in the lowest corner of the slab, and tall pottery jars filled with water flanked it on all sides. Off in an alcove, a small portion of the room was walled off, the entrance hidden by a curtain.

"Before my bath, I must…" Hattie faltered to a stop. Where was the toilet? *Was* there a toilet? Hattie added modern bathroom facilities to her mental checklist of things she missed already.

Nesi appeared to understand. She led Hattie to the alcove and thrust open the curtain. Inside, what appeared to be a hand-carved wooden toilet seat teetered precariously atop two piles of mud bricks. Directly under the hole in the seat was a large bowl, half-filled with sand. A basket next to the seat was also filled with sand and had a scoop of some type thrust into it.

Nesi looked at Hattie questioningly. When she merely lowered her eyebrows and frowned, Nesi pantomimed sitting on the seat, then scooping fresh sand into the bowl underneath. Hattie rolled her eyes. It looked like the best bathroom facilities in the country were the equivalent of a cat-box. Oh, what she wouldn't give for her own cozy bathroom complete with glassed-in tiled shower, fluffy towels, and heat lamp! Sighing, she shooed Nesi away and resigned herself to her fate.

When she finished, Hattie returned to the larger portion of the room where Nesi patiently awaited her.

"Majesty?" Nesi gestured toward the slab. Hattie stepped onto it and before she could say a word, Nesi grabbed the linen sheet she had wrapped around her and whisked it away.

"What are you doing?" Hattie cried.

"Your bath, Majesty," Nesi said simply. She picked up one of the tall jars and upended it over Hattie's head, sending a waterfall of lukewarm water gushing over her.

"This is not a bath…this is a shower!" Hattie sputtered in shock. "And a cold one at that."

Nesi was silent.

"Where is the...um..." Confused, she lapsed into English. "Soap?"

"Soap, Majesty?" Nesi was plainly puzzled. "What is soap?"

"Cleaner? Detergent? You rub it on your skin and it cleans you?"

Nesi shook her head. "I am sorry, Majesty, I know not..."

"Never mind, never mind," Hattie sighed. "Pour the next one more slowly, will you?"

Nesi poured, and Hattie scrubbed, until all the jars were empty. Nesi produced piles of snowy linen towels and rubbed Hattie's body until it glowed, then massaged sweetly scented oil into her skin.

She led Hattie back to the bedroom and dressed her in the scandalous transparent gown that left one breast bare. Hattie almost objected, but her common sense took over. Such gowns were customary here, and if she made a fuss, she would stand out as an intruder. Besides, it didn't seem like her own body that was scandalously clad. It still felt like the body of a stranger. Who was she to complain if Hatshepsut chose to dress in this fashion?

Nesi slipped leather sandals on Hattie's feet, clasped bands of gold around her upper arms and fastened a necklace made of lapis lazuli and gold beads around her neck. Then she gestured for Hattie to sit on the stool.

Hattie sat while Nesi created row upon row of intricate braids in her hair. Next, she took several alabaster pots and ivory sticks from one of the baskets and proceeded to draw thick lines of black kohl along Hattie's eyebrows and above her eyelids all the way out to her temples, matched by lines of green kohl under her eyes. She reddened her cheeks and lips with rouge, and then held up a small, highly polished bronze mirror for Hattie's inspection.

The reflection was a little fuzzy and indistinct, but staring back at her Hattie saw an exotic beauty with an oval face, high forehead, deep brown, almond-shaped eyes, and a delicate pointed chin.

"You are pleased, Majesty?" Nesi asked.

"Oh, aye...Nesi, I am very pleased," Hattie breathed, tearing her eyes away from the mirror. She had just been given the most complete makeover any woman ever experienced. How could she be anything but pleased?

"Come then, Majesty. I will lead you to the throne room."

Suddenly, an enormous snake of panic slithered through the pit of her stomach. Playing at dress-up was one thing. Serving as the ruler of an entire country was another. What if she did something wrong? Could she make a mistake big enough to change history? Was it even *possible* to change history? Hattie moaned. Why had she only skimmed the books on ancient Egypt that Tom had pressed on her? If only she'd paid more attention! A sheen of sweat broke out across her forehead. She should have looked for the necklace instead of the clothing and maybe she'd have been home by now.

"Majesty?"

Hattie clenched her fists. She was trapped, and there was no way out. Holding her head high, she followed Nesi out of the room. She felt as if she were climbing the scaffold to her own execution.

CHAPTER 6

Nesi wound her way through a maze of corridors, Hattie close on her heels. She knew if she lost sight of Nesi for an instant, she'd be lost. At every twist and turn, in every doorway, painted and scantily-clad Egyptians bowed low as she passed. She tried not to let them terrify her, nodding in what she hoped was a regal manner. She had no idea if that was the correct response.

At last, Nesi stopped in front of a tall set of double doors guarded by two fierce-looking men with spears. "Majesty," she said, then slipped away, leaving Hattie to her doom.

Hattie's stomach twisted as she watched the servant's retreating back. She wanted to call to Nesi, tell her to wait, but her mouth felt as though it were stuffed with cotton.

The guards snapped to attention and saluted, spears upright in their left hands, right hands fisted and across their chests; then they threw open the doors. An official dressed in a fine white linen kilt and gold neck and armbands bowed and ushered her in. Striking his long staff against the floor, he announced her presence to the room full of strangers. "King's Great Wife, King's Daughter, King's Sister, God's Wife of Amun, Lady of the Two Lands, Her Majesty Hatshepsut!"

Every painted eye and bewigged head in the room swiveled to her and stared. A sudden impulse seized her to turn and run, screaming, from the palace. Surely, living in the Egyptian desert couldn't be as trying as this?

Hattie forced the impulse down with difficulty. The only hope she had of returning to her own time was to play the part she'd been thrust into, and play it well enough to be above suspicion.

32

Holding her head high, she commanded her shaky legs to carry her, step by agonizing step, to the twin thrones on a raised dais at the opposite end of the room. When she reached them, she paused. Where was she supposed to sit? Would she create a furor if she sat in the wrong one?

The courtier at the end of the room cried out, "His Majesty, King's Son, Prince Tuthmosis!"

A young boy slouched into the room through a side door. So, this was the heir that the ghost—or the hallucination?—had spoken of. He was about eight years old, dressed in a white kilt, his head shaved except a long forelock hanging down on one side. He had a low forehead, a long, narrow face, and small ears. His front teeth stuck out, an effect he tried to counter by keeping his lips pressed tightly shut. *A pity he hadn't been born thirty-five hundred years later*, Hattie thought sympathetically. *Braces would do wonders for him.*

He slumped down on the throne on the left. Wonderful! At least she knew which throne was hers now. Hattie took a seat and turned to the boy. "Good morning, Tuthmosis," she said, smiling brightly.

The boy glanced at her and then turned away. "Stepmother." He nodded, keeping his lips pressed tightly over his teeth.

"What is the matter? Did you get up on the wrong side of the bed?" she inquired pleasantly, still smiling.

He stared at her wide-eyed from under raised brows. "Which side is the wrong side?"

"Never mind, never mind. I am sorry about your father. You must be very sad." She put her hand gently on his arm.

A tear rolled down one cheek and he pulled his arm away. "I am a man now and will be pharaoh one day," he declared stoutly. "I do not need any pity."

Her heart went out to the boy. He was obviously trying so hard to bear up under his grief, and his adult responsibilities as heir to the throne. Hattie reached out to him again, but any words she might have spoken were cut short by a commotion at the other end of the room. The double doors opened again and two men—one in a ragged, stained tunic and the other wearing a fringed leather kilt and helmet—were ushered in by a shaven-headed, rotund, well-dressed priest. The courtier who had announced Hattie rushed up the aisle ahead of the three men. Out of the corner of her eye, Hattie saw Senemut slip into the back of the room. Instantly, she felt as if a weight had been lifted from her shoulders and she sighed deeply. He winked at her and she grinned back.

"Your Majesty Hatshepsut, Prince Tuthmosis, I place before you the soldier Ahmose and Merisu, a potter of Thebes. They are accompanied by Hapuseneb, High Priest of Amun," the courtier announced.

The priest strode arrogantly up to the throne and bowed low. "Majesties, I have brought these men before your royal highnesses for your judgment. May Amun guide your hearts." He stepped back.

Hattie glanced quickly at Tuthmosis. He was staring at a spot over the priest's head, obviously bored. "You may proceed," she said, hoping it was close to the correct response.

The priest pointed to the potter. "Speak."

Merisu stepped forward, then threw himself to the floor at Hattie's feet in abject terror.

"Rise," Hattie said softly. "Do not be afraid. You may speak."

Merisu glanced up and she smiled at him encouragingly. He stood and began his tale in a halting voice. "Oh, Divine One, I have a…a small workshop on the outskirts of the city where I make pottery. Very fine pottery," he added diffidently.

Hattie nodded. "I am sure it is."

"On the fifth day of the first month of inundation, this soldier…" He stopped to gesture timidly at Ahmose. "He came into my workshop. My daughter was there, and he spoke to her in a most disrespectful manner, pressing his attentions upon her. When I protested—for my daughter is unmarried, and has been well brought up—he grew angry, and dashed to the floor every pot and bowl in the shop. He struck me and chased my daughter, screaming, from my sight. She feared to come home until after nightfall. Majesty, I have asked him to recompense me for the damage, but he refuses." The man glanced again at Hattie, and then backed away quickly, bowing and trembling.

"What do you have to say for yourself?" she said, pointing at the soldier Ahmose.

Ahmose swaggered forward. "Majesties, this potter was most rude to me." He jabbed his thumb disdainfully in Merisu's direction. "He offended me, refusing my advances to his daughter. I had thought to honor her with my attention, but she was not pretty enough to be worth the insult I was forced to bear. He received what he deserved. I owe him nothing." He nodded at Hattie and Tuthmosis, then stepped confidently back to his place.

Hapuseneb, the priest, came forward, a self-satisfied smirk on his round face. "Your Majesties can surely see how noble Ahmose has been wronged. This lowly potter has affronted—"

"I can see no such thing." Hattie cut him short, holding up her hand. She glanced at Tuthmosis. He stared up at the ceiling, apparently having nothing to say. She sighed and continued. "What I see is an arrogant soldier who is accustomed to getting what he wants, and is not willing to take responsibility for his own actions. I find no nobility in the man's wanton treatment of the potter and his daughter. Ahmose, it is my judgment that you shall pay Merisu the fair market value for his property that you destroyed."

Ahmose stared at her, his mouth hanging open. The priest sputtered indignantly, "But, Majesty, surely—"

"And," she continued, narrowing her eyes, her voice soft and steely, "you will count yourself lucky, Ahmose, that I do not punish you further for your unjustifiable assault upon this man and his child. See that it does not happen again. That is all."

Several gasps sounded in the room, and were just as quickly stifled. Ahmose blanched, his tanned skin turning sickly pale. Bowing deeply, he hastened from the room. After a final hostile glance, the priest, too, left without a word.

Merisu cleared his throat. "Thank you, Most Radiant One. You are truly the voice of Maat, goddess of justice." He turned and fled the room as if demons pursued him.

Hattie glanced at Tuthmosis. He had paid but scant attention to the proceedings, instead toying with the protective amulet fastened to his left wrist and staring around the room. Suddenly, he noticed that the hearing was over, rose from his throne and withdrew hastily, without a parting word or backward glance.

Sighing, she turned from the sight of his stiff retreating back and found Senemut's gaze upon her. He nodded at her, approval written in every line of his straight, well-muscled body. Relieved that someone agreed with her course of action, she smiled in return. The audience was over.

Hattie had met the young crown prince, given a potter justice, made mortal enemies of a soldier and a priest, and pleased little Neferure's tutor. Not bad, she reflected, for her first official duty as regent and co-ruler of Egypt.

* * *

"By the sacred eye of Horus!" Hapuseneb paced back and forth in his small, secluded chamber in the temple of Amun at Karnak. "That woman is impossible! I cannot tolerate her interference any longer. Did you see the way she upbraided Ahmose in front of the entire court?" He turned to glare at Great Army General Snefru, who slumped on a low stool, his long legs stretched out before him.

"Aye," Snefru muttered. "He is one of my best soldiers. It was unforgivable."

Hapuseneb tapped his upper lip thoughtfully. "We must do something now, before she gets any further out of hand. Who knows what she will take it into her head to do next?"

"I agree." Snefru rose. "Command me, and I shall obey. We must rid Egypt of her swiftly, like routing an enemy in battle. What do you have in mind?"

"You must be patient." Hapuseneb smiled thinly, coldly.

Trained as a soldier, Snefru chafed at inactivity like a bored child. But in his long years of service as a priest, Hapuseneb had learned the advantages of outward composure and waiting for the auspicious moment to act.

"We shall be rid of her before long, I vow. Then, with no other member of the royal family to serve as Regent for the boy, I, High Priest of Amun, shall be appointed Regent and the rule of Egypt will be mine."

CHAPTER 7

"Blast!"

Hattie searched again through the glittering jewels spread across the bed, but it wasn't there. Scores of necklaces, earrings, bracelets, circlets, anklets, and rings lay tangled together, all so beautiful they took her breath away. Not one remotely resembled the pectoral necklace she had been copying when she was somehow thrust into Hatshepsut's body and life.

Though she had no proof, Hattie believed that the necklace—or the hieroglyphics on it—was responsible for her sudden, inexplicable trip to ancient Egypt. She knew she was incapable of remembering and faithfully reproducing all the hieroglyphics, since they were no more meaningful to her than Sanskrit. She was equally certain that, without the necklace, she would be unable to return to her own time. That necklace was as close as she'd ever get to a time machine, and she had to find it. One more cold bath and she would have to throttle someone.

Impatiently, she scooped the jewels back into the basket and clapped her hands. Nesi popped into the room. "Nesi, send His Lordship Senemut to me at once," Hattie requested, waving her away.

In a moment, Senemut strode in. "Majesty," he said, bowing deeply.

"Hattie," she corrected.

He grinned. "Hattie."

Her heart leapt in her chest at the sight of his smile. God, he was the most beautiful man she'd ever seen—sun-bronzed, muscled, with the grace of a panther and the smooth manners of a courtier. What could it hurt if she…but no. She shook herself out of her rosy haze. She needed to keep her mind on her goal of getting home again.

"Senemut, is there another place where Hatshep…I mean, where I keep my jewelry?"

Senemut frowned. "I do not believe so." He searched her face. "Is something missing? Shall I alert the guards?"

"That will not be necessary." She waved away the idea. "But I could have sworn there was another necklace…"

"Mayhap if you would describe it to me?" he suggested.

Hattie pursed her lips, trying to recall the details. "It was a pectoral collar with a golden figure of Horus the falcon. His wings were made of turquoise, lapis lazuli, gold and colored glass beads." She sighed. "It was the most lovely thing I have ever seen." A sudden thought occurred to her. She clapped her hands and sent Nesi to fetch some papyrus, an inkpot and brush.

Nesi returned shortly with the requested items. Hattie seized the brush and dipped it into the inkpot. It felt so good to hold a brush in her hand again! For the first time since this whole affair had begun, she felt like herself. She quickly sketched the outline of the necklace, minus the hieroglyphs, and held it up for Senemut's examination. "There were hieroglyphs here," she said, pointing to the empty spot on the falcon's body.

Senemut opened his eyes wider. "I did not know you possessed such skills with a brush!"

"Ah well…" Hattie shrugged nonchalantly. "It is just a pastime, nothing more. So, do you recognize it?"

He frowned. "I do not recall such a necklace. However, if you wish, I will send for the royal jeweler. He can surely fashion for you a necklace just as you picture. Or mayhap it was a necklace belonging to the Great God, or the Great God's father? Horus is the protector of pharaoh."

"Nay, I do not think it belonged to my husband." She dropped onto the bed in gloomy silence. Tom told her the necklace had *probably* belonged to Hatshepsut. But what if it hadn't? What if it had belonged to some other ancient Egyptian noblewoman or queen—or even, as Senemut suggested, a pharaoh? It might have been buried with a pharaoh centuries ago, or might not yet exist. She could be stuck here, marooned in the past forever, unable to get her hands on the only thing that could save her.

But if the necklace hadn't belonged to Hatshepsut, then how could it have sent her back into Hatshepsut's life? Wouldn't she have traveled to the life of the necklace's real owner? How did time machines work anyway? It was so confusing. It seemed that, in addition to studying ancient Egyptian history, she was remiss in not reading more science fiction.

Senemut said that Horus was the protector of pharaoh. Hatshepsut was not yet pharaoh. If the necklace did belong to her, would Hattie have to wait—months, years?—until Hatshepsut was crowned pharaoh for the necklace to appear?

Hattie knew she could have a necklace produced to her specifications, thereby obtaining an excellent copy of the piece Tom had showed her. But she would never be able to duplicate the hieroglyphics. She didn't know how to read them, so she had no idea what had been inscribed on the figure of the falcon. And the hieroglyphs, she was certain, were the key to the mystery. They must be some kind of charm or incantation that had sent her hurtling to the past. Perhaps if she learned to read hieroglyphics, she could remember those on the necklace? It was worth a try.

"I feel your sorrow." Senemut's concerned voice pierced her grim thoughts. "It floats around you like a cloud. What can I do to lighten your heart?"

She looked up at him. She couldn't tell him the truth…not yet anyway. She was still an outcast here, who could be tortured in nasty ways or even executed if found to be an imposter. "I know not what to do. I am Regent, yet I do not understand what is expected of me. I do not belong here. Tuthmosis will not accept my help, and I feel useless."

"Is that all?" He smiled gently down on her.

"That is enough."

"Aye, well, then it is easily explained. The young prince has recently lost his father. You have been made his regent, as he is obviously too young to rule. Yet, you are not the boy's mother, but only his stepmother. Of course, he is trying to hide his emotions from you and behave as he believes a man should."

"Aye, I suppose you must be right." Hattie brightened. "As you have said, I am only his stepmother. Who is his mother? Could she not serve as Regent for her son, instead of me?"

Senemut's eyes widened in shock and he stepped back a pace. "The prince's mother is Lady Isis, one of the lesser wives in your royal husband's harem. She is lowborn and uneducated. She has no training to rule Egypt. Surely, Your Majesty knows that she is totally unsuitable."

"Of course, of course. I had forgotten," Hattie placated him. It seemed all she could do was put her foot in her mouth! "You are right."

"You are the daughter of the king," he continued. "You are of royal blood. It is your duty to serve as Tuthmosis's regent."

"Aye, I suppose it is." She sighed. "Well, then, I intend to befriend the boy. If I am to rule with him, I would like the relationship to be amicable."

"May I suggest that you send young Tuthmosis away to train with the army? The discipline would be good for him. It might give him the maturity he lacks, and it will teach him respect for authority. Hapuseneb, the high priest, agrees with me."

"The army? At his age? He is just a boy! Nay, I do not think that is a good idea." She shook her head. "There must be another way to make him more amenable without banishing him."

"As you wish, Majesty," Senemut said stiffly, a touch of disapproval in his tone. "But I fear it will be more difficult than you foresee."

"Mayhap you are right. Oh, Senemut, I know not what to do! If you are angry with me, then I have no one to turn to." She had to be careful...she couldn't afford to alienate her only friend in this time.

His expression softened. "I am not angry, Hattie. I wish to help you in any way I can. Surely you know that."

"Then sit with me, please." She gestured to the stool. "I need to ask you something."

"Ask me anything you wish." He pulled the stool close to the bed and sat down.

"I want you to serve as my…my advisor," she said slowly, watching his face as she spoke. "I need someone I can rely on, someone close to me whom I can trust. My memory is still faulty from my illness." She winced at the white lie she was forced to tell him. But he would never accept the truth about her origin. Would he? And she didn't yet know him well enough to trust him with her life.

"I am honored you feel you can rely on me, and I will happily assist you in any way I can," he answered, his expression grave. "But I must spend many hours each day tutoring Neferure. Mayhap someone else could assist you? Ineni or Ahmose-Pennekheb? They both served your royal husband faithfully."

She shook her head. "There is no one else I trust. It must be you. Someone new can be found to tutor the princess, is that not so?"

Senemut smiled at her and her heart stopped. "Of course, if Your Majesty wishes. Might I suggest Senimen to tutor the little one? She likes him well enough, and he is most eager to advance in your service."

"Good! It is settled then. Inform him in the morning. And now, you shall be my advisor." She sighed. "You have no idea how relieved and grateful I am." She reached out impulsively and took his hand.

At first, he attempted to jerk his hand away, but Hattie clasped it firmly, not allowing him to pull back. After a moment, he squeezed her hand, covering it with both of his.

Heat coursed through her body. She was the queen, and no one dared touch her except her servant, Nesi. Even Senemut would not presume to be so forward, save in moments of dire need. She hadn't realized until this moment how starved she was for human contact, the touch of a man's hand. She clung to him.

He raised his other hand to her face, hesitated, and then stroked her cheek, his eyes never leaving hers. His caress was feather-light, yet she felt it in every fiber of her body. She was drowning in his gaze.

"Senemut," she breathed. "Senemut, I…" She reached out to

him with her free hand, then shook herself and gently extracted her fingers from his. This was no time to get lost in a romantic haze—she had work to do. "We must make your position official. You need a title, so no one can question your authority. What do you suggest?"

Senemut's face looked like a sleeper's, awakening from a dream. "I know not…whatever Your Majesty wishes," he said, his voice low and husky.

"Hattie, please," she murmured.

"Aye. Hattie. In private," he amended. "I dare not take such liberties in public."

"Very well…for the present," she said. "Your title must be above reproach. There must be no one higher than you. You must be my most revered advisor. No one must be able to countermand you, save me. I know not what the title should be, Senemut. Advise me."

"Hattie, are you truly unable to recall?"

"Aye, I am afraid it is true."

"Then, you must name me Steward of Amun, though I hesitate to suggest such an honor." He bowed his head.

"Steward of Amun?" Hattie frowned. "That does not sound important enough. Steward sounds like the title of a household servant. Are you certain that will do?"

"I assure you, it is the most important position in the two lands, save only High Priest of Amun and, of course, Pharaoh."

"Very well, then. Steward of Amun you shall be, my most trusted advisor, and—" She raised his chin gently and smiled into his eyes. "—my friend."

CHAPTER 8

"Steward of Amun! Can you believe it?" Hapuseneb asked bitterly, spinning around to face the general across the small room.

He knew the answer before Snefru gave it. The fury was plainly marked on the soldier's face.

"It is preposterous! I should have been named steward. Did I not faithfully serve His Majesty Tuthmosis, father of Hatshepsut, for years?" Snefru snapped, halting long enough in his pacing to glare at the priest.

"The man is common-born and completely unsuitable," Hapuseneb went on. Snefru was a good partner in conspiracy, but had a short attention span. Keeping his anger white-hot was a little security measure that Hapuseneb had every intention of using to its fullest advantage. "But what can one expect with a soft-hearted woman as Regent? His handsome face has turned her head. Pah!" He shook his head in disgust. "We must do something about her. She is dangerous and she has become a liability."

"Aye, so you say. But words accomplish nothing. When do we act?"

"Watch your tongue," Hapuseneb growled. "I do not need commands from you, only loyalty. I will think of something soon, something that will not fail, and we shall be rid of her. And the usurper Senemut also."

* * *

Hori bowed as he entered Senemut's office. "You wished to see me, Lord?" Clucking his tongue disapprovingly, he hastened to light the lamp. "Why sit you here in the dark?"

Senemut looked up from the papyrus he absently rolled and unrolled. "I am sorry. I did not realize that night was upon us.

Please, Hori, sit with me." He gestured at a stool to his right. "I have news and I wish you to be the first to hear it."

Hori grinned. "It is my pleasure." He seated himself gingerly and heaved a deep sigh of contentment. "What is the news?"

Senemut stifled a smile. Hori's rheumatism troubled him more frequently these days, yet he refused to slow down or relinquish any of his duties. So Senemut found as many excuses as he could to insist that the older man sit and rest. "I have been granted a new title and position by Her Gracious Majesty Hatshepsut."

"Oh, have you?" Hori's eyes were bright with curiosity. "And what title did Her Majesty see fit to confer upon you?"

"It is a most honorable one," Senemut said, drawing out the tale and watching Hori from the corner of his eye. "She suggested it this morning. Of course, I told her I was unworthy of such great favor."

"Unworthy? By Amun, it had best be worthy of *you* or I will…" Hori leaned forward, fists clenched.

"Oh, it is most prestigious, Hori, I vow," Senemut said, laughing. "Do not fear; she has offered no insults to your once-wayward charge."

Hori cuffed him lightly, then leaned back and folded his arms. "Shame on you for provoking an old man! End the suspense, I pray, and tell me your news before I expire of vexation."

"Very well," Senemut said, still chuckling. "I will torment you no further. Hatshepsut has named me Steward of Amun."

Hori gasped, his eyes wide. "Steward of Amun? Truly?"

Senemut nodded. "She will assign Senimen to tutor little Neferure. That will free me to be her closest advisor, to assist her in any fashion I may."

Hori clapped his hands. "I have known since your childhood that you were destined for greatness. But I dared not believe you would rise so high! Praise Amun for his bounty."

"Aye, well, you have always held great aspirations on my behalf. No man could ask for a more enthusiastic advocate," Senemut said. "I did not believe this was possible, since I am not of noble birth. I must confess I am still mystified by it."

"Why?" Hori narrowed his eyes. "Has someone implied you

are not qualified for the position?"

"Oh, I am most certainly qualified." Senemut shook his head and frowned. "Nay, it is Her Majesty who continues to mystify me."

"In what way? Is she still confused, still having problems with her memory?"

"Nay, she seems more decisive now. Her memory is improving, though she still asks questions on occasion that she should know the answer to. But her judgments are…well, they seem most unlike her." He spread his hands. "I know not how to describe it."

"What decision of Her Majesty's do you find so unusual?"

"Well…" Senemut paused, then grinned. "Of course, there is the matter of my unexpected advancement in her service. But we have already discussed my aptness for the position." He leaned forward and motioned Hori closer. "This morning, Her Majesty suggested…" He looked around the room swiftly. "You must swear to reveal this to no one, Hori. Swear!"

"Aye, I swear," Hori said, gesturing irritably. "Get on with it."

"Very well. I will hold you to your word." Senemut dropped his voice. "Her Majesty suggested that the Lady Isis serve as regent for Tuthmosis."

Hori reared back in horror. "By the sacred eye of Horus! Is this true?"

Senemut nodded. "Of course, I told Her Majesty that the Lady Isis is common-born and not suitable to serve as regent. Her Majesty did not insist, so that brought an end to the discussion. Still, I am worried," he murmured, his mind turning from Hori to Hatshepsut.

What was the explanation for her eccentric behavior? Was she still ill? Amun help her, had the illness affected her mind as well as her body?

"What do you suggest I do, Hori?" he added. "I am worried about Hattie. I wish to be of as much help to her as…"

"Hattie?" Hori eyed him shrewdly. "How is it you call Her Glorious Majesty by a pet name of childhood?"

Senemut looked at Hori, and then dropped his glance under the older man's perceptive gaze. "I…that is…Her Majesty requested I address her thus. In private," he added, to soften the words.

"I like it not." Hori sat back and scowled. "It is dangerous to befriend royalty. I have lived a long time, Senemut, and I cannot begin to count the number of *friends* of pharaoh who have disappeared suddenly and never been seen again—except in small, unidentifiable chunks that wash up on the shores of the Nile! I do not wish the same to happen to you."

"Nor do I wish to grace the belly of a crocodile." Senemut shuddered. "Yet Hattie—Her Majesty—says she has need of me. She seems so lonely, so dazed, so confused since the death of her husband, the Great God. How can I refuse a request from her?" Then, he continued more softly, "And I am not sure I *wish* to refuse her anything she requests."

Hori shook his head. "This bodes ill for you, I fear. You are falling in love with her…nay, do not trouble yourself to deny it! It is writ clearly across your face—as clear as Ra shines above." He pointed at Senemut. "Mark me well…no good can come of this."

Senemut sighed. "You may be right, old friend, but I am as powerless to halt it as I am the flow of the Nile. I am under her spell, and naught can change that. She holds my heart in her hands."

CHAPTER 9

"Make this stroke a little longer," Senemut urged, leaning over Hattie's shoulder. "Do not forget to add the *ankh*. There! You have done it correctly. You have written your name: Hatshepsut."

Hattie dropped the brush and picked up the scrap of papyrus, scrutinizing it. The hieroglyphs were a bit straggly, but they were recognizable. Her training as an artist had paid off. She sighed with pleasure. "I thank you for your help, Senemut! I cannot believe that I must learn to write again. My memory has played me false," she said, then winced, a little alarmed at how easily the lie now came to her lips.

"You are learning rapidly, Hattie. It is a pleasure to have such an apt pupil. And such a beautiful one," he added, smiling.

Hattie stared at him, her cheeks growing warm. "Why, Senemut! I believe this is the first time you have paid me a compliment. I thank you."

The laugh lines around his eyes grew deeper as his smile broadened. "You have been forthright with me, and have honored me with your trust. I am glad to give you my trust in return, and speak to you the words of my heart."

Hattie groaned inwardly. She trusted Senemut implicitly, it was true, yet she had not given him the complete truth in return. She hadn't told him who she really was, or how she came to be there. Instead, she'd stuck to the glib lie that now came so easily out of her mouth. She longed to tell him the truth, but didn't dare. The truth was too fantastic for the most educated twenty-first century mind to accept. How could she expect Senemut to believe it?

On the other hand, ancient Egypt was rife with belief in

47

magic, spells and incantations, and the inexplicable doings of gods and goddesses. Perhaps Senemut would have little trouble accepting her bizarre tale as fact. Didn't she owe it to him to give him the opportunity to know and embrace the truth? Had she underestimated him?

Hattie cleared her throat. "Senemut, I have something I must tell you—"

A messenger burst into the room at that moment and dropped to his knees, cutting short her faltering confession. "Majesty!" he cried. "Forgive my intrusion. I bear a most important message!" He halted, panting, looking from Hattie to Senemut and back again.

Hattie glanced at Senemut, then turned to the messenger. "Very well. Give me the message."

The messenger rose and passed a papyrus scroll to her. "It is from the Great Army General Snefru, Majesty."

She unrolled the scroll and scrutinized it. Her reading ability was still far too new to allow her to decipher it accurately. Silently, she passed the scroll to Senemut.

Senemut scanned the papyrus, then turned to the messenger. "You may go."

The messenger bowed and hastened from the room.

Senemut turned to Hattie, his expression grave. "Snefru says that Nubia is rebelling. He awaits your orders."

Hattie was in over her head with the intricacies of local politics. Geography had never been her strong suit, even in her own time, and here all the countries bore unfamiliar names. "Nubia is rebelling? Why? I do not understand."

"A change of pharaohs is often viewed as an opportunity to rebel—because the reins of power are held a little slackly at such times, or mayhap just to test the mettle of the new ruler. It is best to crush such uprisings quickly, before they get out of hand." His voice was harsh.

"Crush the uprising? I do not like the sound of that. Could we not send an ambassador to negotiate for peace? Chancellor Neshi, mayhap?"

"The time for diplomacy is past," Senemut insisted. "The Nubians are a vassal state, and have no authority to rebel against their rulers. It is vital that Egypt defend and maintain her borders, her territory. If one such rebellion is overlooked, every vassal state will soon rebel. It must be stopped at once. I feel certain Chancellor Neshi would agree with me."

Fear and indecision gripped Hattie. She was certain the real Hatshepsut would have spent a lifetime in training for this moment, and would know exactly what to do. She would have no qualms about ordering troops into action, and having those troops slaughter every last man, woman and child who dared to attempt to throw off her rule. Wasn't that the way it worked in antiquity?

But Hattie hadn't been trained and educated for that. She wasn't a fearless warrior. She was simply an artist, sadly out of her depth in the mysteries and intrigues of an ancient, bloodthirsty world.

A fragrant breeze caressed her cheek. Startled, she looked around for the source. It was a hot, windless day, as were most days in Egypt. The curtain over her door didn't move, yet she felt the sensation again—this time, more strongly. It was like the presence she had felt in the museum, the voice that urged her to touch the necklace. "Trust Senemut," the ethereal voice whispered.

Hattie whipped around. She and Senemut were the only ones in the room. She strode to the door and jerked open the curtain. The hallway was empty. Was she going crazy? Or had the mysterious voice followed her from her own time?

"What is it, Hattie?" Senemut's voice broke in on her thoughts.

Turning back to face him, she sighed. "Nothing, nothing. I just thought I heard…never mind." She dismissed it with a wave of her hand. Regardless of the source of the voice—her subconscious or a ghost—the advice was sound. She had to rely on Senemut's counsel and her own commonsense to guide her in this crisis. She had no choice.

"I agree Nubia's rebellion must be put down," she told him. "What do you suggest?"

"You must crush the uprising," he repeated.

"Aye, but how? I mean, how many troops shall I send? What kind of equipment? What about a battle plan? What shall I tell General Snefru? You agreed to be my advisor, Senemut. I need your recommendations."

"I see. Very well. I would suggest…" He paused and pursed his lips. "I suggest you send six hosts of infantry and charioteers, together with their horses and equipment, up the Nile to quell the uprising at once. That should be sufficient. Tell the general to accept nothing less than total surrender. He will know what to do."

"Aye, that seems logical, I suppose. You are certain there is no way to avoid bloodshed?"

Senemut slowly shook his head.

Hattie sighed with resignation. "All right, it shall be done. But no women and children are to be killed—only soldiers. I want that made perfectly clear."

"I do not think that is wise. The Nubians must be shown that they dare not rebel against the forces of Egypt." His jaw tightened. "Mercy will only convince them you are weak, and they will try again."

Hattie shook her head. "This point is not negotiable. No women and children will be killed. That is my order."

"As you wish." Senemut looked unconvinced. "There is one other point. It is customary for pharaoh to lead his troops into battle. Of course, Tuthmosis is too small and you are…well, under these circumstances, Snefru will lead the troops. He will—"

"Why do you think I would shrink from my duty?" she interrupted. Her stomach quivered wildly and her heart pounded, but she was determined to fulfill the role that had been thrust upon her. If she were to live Hatshepsut's life, even for a short space of time, she must live it the way Hatshepsut would. She had no right to change things to suit her own twenty-first century sensibilities. Besides, what would happen if she changed the course that history had followed? Would she be unable to return to her own time, marooned forever in the past? She shuddered at the thought. "If it is customary for pharaoh to lead the troops, then as Regent, I shall do so. And you shall accompany me."

Senemut stared at her, his eyes narrowed. A frown etched lines in his forehead. She matched him stubbornly look for look and waited an endless moment to hear his reply. What if he refused to go with her to Nubia? She needed his help and advice—she knew nothing about combat tactics and battle strategies. She did not dare make a fool of herself in front of her soldiers.

Even worse, what if he laughed at the thought of a woman as head of the armed forces? In her own time, women still struggled for equality in the military, and in antiquity, a female soldier was nearly unheard of. If she couldn't win *his* respect, she had no hope of commanding a division of soldiers. Everything depended on him.

At last, his gaze softened. He lifted his hand to his shoulder in a salute. "Fierce little warrior," he murmured. "It will be my very great honor to accompany the Lady of the Two Lands into battle. And I swear upon my eternal ka, I will protect you with my life."

Hattie swallowed convulsively over the large lump that had suddenly materialized in her throat. She took his hand and kissed the palm swiftly. "Send the message, Senemut. Then come to my chambers. We have many preparations to make and a battle to plan."

* * *

"The favor of the gods is with us," Hapuseneb said, rubbing his hands together. "She has decided to lead the troops herself into battle against the Nubians. With any luck, our problem will be taken care of for us by Egypt's enemies. What delicious irony! I could not have planned it better myself. I should thank the Nubians for rebelling." He grinned. "But, of course, your carefully placed rumors of a weak woman on the throne gave them the… push they needed to decide the time was right for an uprising."

"How did she come to this decision to lead the battle herself?" Snefru asked, lounging arrogantly in a carved wooden chair in Hapuseneb's chamber. "I am astonished, I admit. Hatshepsut was ever a meek, timid woman. This is not like her."

"I did not need soil my hands. That traitor, Senemut, must have convinced Her Majesty to go. Little does he know that, in his own bumbling way, he is serving *our* ends." Hapuseneb was pleased now that he had drawn Snefru into the conspiracy. Snefru could oversee the Nubian campaign personally, and make sure that

Hatshepsut met with a fatal mishap. Such things were regrettable, but they happened often on the field of battle and thus would not be deemed suspicious.

Snefru nodded. "Aye! And when we are rid of her, we shall rid ourselves of him as well. Then you will rule Egypt, through the boy, and I shall be Steward of Amun. Together, we will conquer the world!"

The two men laughed, then raised their wine goblets in toast to the gods.

CHAPTER 10

With Senemut at her side, Hattie left her cabin in the center of the two-hundred-foot ship, moved past the oarsmen rowing, and leaned over the railing next to the intricately carved arched prow of the *Avenging Falcon*. She amused herself by watching the sparkling waters of the Nile slip silently past. After a few minutes a moderate wind arose, the large rectangular sail went up, and the oarsmen found themselves with a respite from their heavy labor.

To Hattie, the trip was a magical interlude, one sleepy sunlit day drifting into the next.

Senemut proved to be a most interesting travel companion, telling story after story of Egypt, her pharaohs, and her people. He seemed to know the story behind every imposing monument and obscure temple they passed. They lounged together at the rail, the days filled with laughter and wonder, while she sketched the oarsmen at work, fishermen casting their nets, farmers working in the fields, crocodiles sprawling on the sandbanks.

And when she caught him unaware, she drew Senemut's profile, outlined against setting sun. At night, in Hattie's cabin, they dined together on fish and honey cakes and drank date wine. She couldn't remember ever having known such happiness, or such peace. She seemed to be living in a dream.

But all sleepers awake, all dreams end, and this one would end shortly. The flotilla of ships would reach the Second Cataract the following day and the great Egyptian fort at Buhen, two hundred miles south of where their journey had begun. Then, the battle would begin in earnest. Hattie rubbed her arms, suddenly chilled despite the stifling afternoon heat.

Preparations for the campaign had been swift. Soldiers were mustered, chariots, horses, equipment, troops, and rowers loaded onto sailing ships, and the journey south to Nubia commenced. The prevailing wind from the north meant that the oarsmen had little work to do, simply resting on their oars and biding their time in case the wind should change or drop.

Only one part of the journey had been difficult. A stretch of rapids at the First Cataract proved much too violent to allow safe passage by ship, forcing the army and crew members to disembark, haul the vessels ashore by brute force, and drag them six miles farther south to bypass the rapids.

Hattie suggested harnessing the horses to the ships and allowing them to help with the task, but General Snefru insisted the horses' strength be saved for the battle. The effects of the close confinement aboard ship would be enough for them to bear.

Senemut tried to convince Hattie to remain aboard the *Avenging Falcon* while the men dragged it past the rapids. She refused. If she expected the generals and common soldiers to respect her, she couldn't afford to project the image of a soft, pampered woman. Instead, she traveled the six miles on foot, braving the sweltering heat and brutal desert sun to march at the head of her soldiers and crewmen, wearing the blue crown of war. Though none dared speak to her, she saw approval shining in her troops' eyes, making every blister and aching muscle a badge of honor. Even Senemut, forced to admit that she was correct, nodded his approval.

Hattie had only one day left in which to rest and mentally prepare for the combat to come. Thinking of the impending battle made her stomach twitch. Trying to divert her thoughts, she turned to Senemut. "Tell me about your childhood. I know little about you. You have told me stories of everyone save yourself."

Senemut smiled. "I fear there is not much to tell. I was born in Armant, south of Thebes. I have three brothers, Amenemhat, Minhotep and Pairy, and two sisters, Ahhotep and Nofret-Hor. We were not wealthy, but we were comfortable. My father saw to it that we each received a good education, the best he could provide.

"I joined the army, participated in a campaign or two, and distinguished myself enough to catch the eye of a highly-placed temple official." He shrugged. "So I was transferred to an administrative position in the temple of Amun at Karnak, where I found favor in the eyes of your husband, the Great God. You know the rest."

No, I don't, Hattie thought. *But I don't dare push my luck by admitting it.* "That sounds so…official. So lonely. Did you not have friends?"

He shook his head. "I had acquaintances. I did not have time for friends."

"And you never married?"

"Nay."

"Why not?"

Senemut turned from his absorbed study of the Nile to look into her eyes. "Because I never found a woman with whom I wanted to share my home and my life. Or mayhap, I never found a woman with whom I *could* share my life."

Hattie tingled all over from the warmth of his gaze. "What do you mean? Surely, you could choose any woman in all Egypt." She smiled. "I have seen the way the noblewomen fawn over you! You could have any of them."

Senemut turned from her with a sigh and responded in a voice so soft, she was not certain whether she heard it with her ears, or with her heart. "Any woman, save the one I desire."

Hattie longed for him with a sudden, fierce ache that she had never felt before. She wanted to seize him, cover his face with kisses, breathe in his scent. She wanted to tell him that she would marry him and bear his children. She reached out to him with a moan, but before she could touch him, she jerked her hand back.

It wasn't fair to become involved with him. She didn't belong in this time, and she had no intention of staying. As soon as she located the necklace, she would do her best to return to the twenty-first century immediately. The last thing she wanted to do was to leave him behind, grieving for her—or worse yet, to find himself suddenly confronted with the real Hatshepsut, a woman who might not be in love with him, who perhaps did not want him in the way he wanted her.

Hattie had no way of knowing what would happen to the body of Hatshepsut when she fled it to return to her own time. She still wasn't certain if the presence she had felt on several occasions was a ghost or her imagination. If a ghost, would Hatshepsut's spirit return from the land of the dead when Hattie returned to Chicago? Rejection might be harder for Senemut to bear than outright loss; neither would be pleasant.

Honesty compelled Hattie to admit she didn't want to grieve for Senemut either. She wanted to return to her tidy, comfortable life with no strings left hanging, nothing out of place. So she vowed to do the sensible thing: avoid getting involved.

As she stared at his rugged profile outlined against the setting sun, her heart gave a painful lurch and a sob caught in her throat. It wouldn't be an easy vow to honor.

* * *

Hattie sat on a stool, shielded from the sun, but not from the heat or the incessant, buzzing flies. Her tent, royal standards hanging sullenly in the motionless air, sat high atop a hill overlooking tomorrow's battlefield, assuring her a commanding view of the entire horrific spectacle.

The sound of hammering, shouted orders and curses, and the whinnies of horses filled the camp. Most of the soldiers worked to set up tents, to put together chariots, or to sharpen spears and swords. Hattie, Senemut, and her generals turned their attention to mapping out their battle plan.

"The Nubians know little of strategy," General Snefru said scornfully. "It should be a simple matter to defeat them. Their only tactic is to rush headlong at the enemy, hacking away with swords and battle axes." A tall, powerfully built man, he strode relentlessly back and forth in the tent. Watching him made Hattie dizzy, and the graphic pictures his words evoked caused her stomach to leap with nausea.

She nodded. "How do we counter their assault?"

He moved closer, pointing to a rough representation of the

battlefield on a scrap of papyrus. "We divide our forces into three segments, Majesty. When the enemy moves forward, two wings of five hundred men each will move around their flanks. Chariots will quickly cut off their route of escape to the rear, while infantry hems them in on both sides. When they are driven inevitably ahead of the chariots, the fifteen hundred soldiers remaining at the center will slaughter them. It will be a glorious victory for Your Majesty!"

She shivered at the all-too-vivid description. There was no way to make war sound glorious, or even respectable. It was a ruthless event, even when undertaken for the best of reasons. She sighed and turned to Senemut. "What do you think?"

He nodded. "It is a sensible plan, Majesty."

"Very well then. Make it so. But there is one thing I insist on."

Snefru, already on his way out of the tent, was brought up short. "Aye, Majesty?"

"There will be no women or children harmed."

"But…but, Majesty!" he cried. "The soldiers have always enjoyed the spoils of war as part of their just reward for battle. Women and children are part of that incentive."

Hattie shook her head stubbornly. "War is brutal enough. I expect my troops to act with the dignity befitting Egyptian soldiers. There will be no killing or raping of women or children. The battle will be honorable, or there will be no battle. Do you understand? See that my orders are obeyed, or the guilty ones will suffer the consequences."

Snefru's eyes widened and he scowled, but he dared not debate further. "Aye, Majesty. It shall be as you wish." He left the tent hastily, casting hostile glances behind him.

"I know not if that was wise, Hattie," Senemut said after Snefru was out of earshot. "It will be difficult to maintain the respect of your army if you appear to be softhearted. Snefru has always believed a weak pharaoh makes for a weak Egypt, which then becomes a target for conquest."

"I am not weak," Hattie retorted. "I am honorable. There is a difference." She subsided into a gloomy silence, wondering if she could indeed call herself honorable, when tomorrow she would send perhaps thousands of men to their deaths. Where was the honor in that?

Dinner was a quiet affair. Hattie picked at her food. She had no appetite. Senemut tried to divert her attention with amusing tales of court gossip and intrigue, but she couldn't concentrate. At last, he gave up.

"Go to bed now, Hattie, and rest. You will need all of your strength in the morning. I will sleep directly outside your tent. You need only call me if you wish anything." He strode out of the tent, fastening the flap securely behind him.

Hattie moaned and sank down onto her cot, fearing that sleep was as far away as twenty-first century Chicago. *Call him if she wished anything?* She wished to spend the night in his arms, safe and secure; she wished to wake and find the impending battle was but a hideous dream; she wished tomorrow would never come. More than anything, she wished she had never been transported back to Hatshepsut's Egypt.

* * *

Yet, Hattie did sleep. And soon Hatshepsut stood, shimmering, before her in the velvet darkness of her dream.

"You," Hattie breathed. "You have to help me! I am no warrior. I cannot lead troops into battle. I cannot wage war!"

Hatshepsut smiled gently. "You have the heart of a warrior, though you lack the training. Trust in Senemut. Trust in the army. They will know what to do."

"But surely a battle will not lead me to the name of the traitor who poisoned you," Hattie protested. "You told me I must fulfill a mission, and then I could go home. But this is not part of my mission!"

"That is not correct," Hatshepsut said, holding up a finger. "True, you are to find the traitor and protect Tuthmosis. But how can you complete your mission if Egypt falls to ruin around your ears? Nay, you must protect Egypt, strengthen her, rule her well until my return. Do not fail me in this."

"Well, I am doing my best," Hattie responded tartly. Her life had been disrupted beyond all reason, but she had tried to adjust to her new role and surroundings; yet Hatshepsut still had the temerity to lecture her? "But I am not a ruler, nor am I a soldier. I am simply an artist, sadly out of her element! Mayhap you should have chosen another, more suitable woman to complete your mission."

Hatshepsut's expression softened and she smiled graciously. "You are the only person who can help me, and I am not ungrateful. It is vital to Egypt—nay, to the world—that Tuthmosis is protected, the traitor caught, history set right. Your mission is critical." She frowned and reached out to Hattie. "But you must be wary. There is evil here, great evil, and you are in danger. Do not relax your vigilance."

"Well, of course there is danger here," Hattie snapped. "I am in the middle of a war zone!"

"The danger comes not from the battle itself," Hatshepsut said. "I feel a presence here, covering all like a malevolent cloud. Mayhap the traitor himself lurks in some shadow. Be alert. Trust no one other than Senemut. He will protect you."

"I trust him, do not fear," Hattie murmured. "I trust him with my life."

"As well you should." Hatshepsut's image shimmered and grew transparent, then vanished. "Protect Egypt and Tuthmosis. Do not fail me," the disembodied voice added.

"Hatshepsut, Egypt, and the world are all depending on me," Hattie muttered as she slipped deeper into sleep. "What more can go wrong?"

CHAPTER 11

The day dawned bright and clear, but the camp had been stirring since well before the sun rose. Hattie surveyed the preparations from her lofty perch atop the hill overlooking the battlefield. Grooms led horses to chariots, soldiers fastened on leather helmets and swords, and officers moved from company to company, giving orders and encouragement. Everything was running smoothly; her help was not needed. The best thing she could do for her troops was to stay out from underfoot.

She glanced across the field of battle as the warm light of dawn spread across the grassy plain. From what she could see, the Nubians were making their preparations at the far end of the field. Combat was inevitable.

She turned to Senemut. "What must I do? Should I ride in a chariot at the head of my troops?"

Wearing a serious expression, he shook his head. "Snefru will come to you when all is in readiness. You must give him the order to proceed. Then, you need only stand on the crest of this hill and watch the battle. It will not take long."

Hattie winced. "I…I confess I am loathe to watch my soldiers die. I cannot help but feel their blood is on my hands."

"You must be strong." He looked around, then unobtrusively reached for her hand. "Your soldiers must see you fearless and brave, urging them on. It will inspire them to fight fiercely."

"I know you are right, and I will stay. You will be here with me, will you not?" She clutched his hand with both of hers.

"Of course."

"Majesty?"

She dropped Senemut's hand and turned to see Snefru striding to her. "Aye, General?"

"All is prepared. I await your orders."

"Very well." She paused, glancing at Senemut, who smiled encouragingly. "Begin the battle. May Sekhmet, goddess of war, grant you and your men a glorious victory."

Snefru saluted sharply and ran to issue the orders.

A sick, uneasy feeling crawled around in the pit of Hattie's stomach as she looked down on her troops. For a brief moment, the scene seemed frozen in time. Chariots and infantry stood in straight lines at the near edge of the field, with the Nubians in a more disorderly clump at the opposite end. Then, at an unheard signal, the battle began.

Hattie's troops marched forward in even rows until the Nubians began to advance on them. Then, wings of infantry swung to the left and right to flank the enemy, while the chariots raced at top speed to work their way behind the Nubians.

The Nubian troops, suddenly sensing the purpose of the unfamiliar flanking strategy, tried to retreat, but it was too late. The horse-drawn chariots had moved into position like lightning, and there was no way out. Resigned, the enemy soldiers turned forward again and launched a violent attack on the troops awaiting their arrival.

Screams and cries, shouted orders and curses, clanging of metal against metal, and the thuds of spear points and bronze-tipped arrows meeting leather shields rose to Hattie's ears on the still, dry air. Dust obscured portions of the scene from time to time, but there was no disguising the amount of hot, red blood being spilled, even from such a great distance. Moaning, Hattie closed her eyes.

At once, she felt Senemut's left arm come around her waist, his right hand cupping her elbow. "Hold your head high, Majesty," he whispered. "Your soldiers are winning for you a great victory. Your name will be written for all the ages."

Gulping, Hattie raised her head and forced herself to open her eyes. If her soldiers were dying for her eternal glory, the least she could do was to provide them with a vision of a fierce, fearless ruler—no matter how false that image felt deep in her heart.

Suddenly, she heard a small sound. It was no louder than the footstep of a servant outside her room in the palace, but it drew her attention. She whipped around to her left and saw a huge Nubian soldier creeping around the corner of her tent, knife upraised as he approached her.

"Senemut!" she cried. She felt rooted to the spot, watching in horror as the attacker broke into a run toward them.

At once, Senemut seized her and shoved her behind him, then turned to face the assassin. "Get away, Hattie!" he shouted to her as he grasped both of the Nubian's forearms with his hands, struggling to keep the knife out of striking distance.

Senemut's warning broke her trance and she stumbled into her tent, looking for something—anything—she could use as a weapon to help him. She had no intention of running away and leaving him to be butchered. Her eyes settled on a large pottery wine jar. Seizing it, she rushed outside.

The men still struggled, both of them covered with dust and sweat. Senemut seized the attacker's knife hand and tried to wrest the weapon from him. They spun around and crashed into a stool outside the tent. Falling in a tangle of flailing limbs, they lost their hold on each other. Hattie stumbled back just in time to avoid being caught in the fracas, somehow managing to keep her grip on the unwieldy wine jar.

They leapt to their feet and faced off again, the Nubian still in possession of the knife. Blood trickled down Senemut's side from a wound the Nubian had inflicted. They panted, sweat gleaming on their heaving chests. The intruder was taller and heavier, but Senemut's lithe body had the grace of a leopard and the muscular power of a lion.

The assassin suddenly charged at Senemut, his head lowered. Senemut darted nimbly out of his path and seized him from behind, pulling the man's arms behind him and forcing him down to his knees. The Nubian cried out in pain and struggled to free himself.

Seizing the opportunity, Hattie raised the heavy jar and smashed it onto the assailant's head with all the strength she could muster. It shattered, wine and pottery shards spraying over both combatants. The Nubian groaned and Senemut released him, letting him slump to the ground.

Senemut bent over, his hands on his knees, breathing harshly. At last he stood upright and faced her. "You…are a fierce warrior… Hattie," he panted. "I thank you for your assistance." He put out his tongue to catch a drip of wine trickling down his face, then grinned. "But I fear…it was a waste of good wine."

Hattie laughed, giddy with relief. "It is I who should thank you. You saved my life."

"It was my duty, Majesty," he said, and bowed. "And my very great pleasure. Have your soldiers won another victory for you yet?" He gestured in the direction of the field of combat.

Hattie looked down at the field below and discovered that, at last, the battle was over. Sounds of conflict dwindled, leaving only the moans and cries of the injured and dying. As predicted, Egypt's seasoned troops had achieved an easy victory over the inexperienced Nubian soldiers. "Aye. It appears to be finished." She turned back to him and gasped. "You are bleeding! Let me take a look at that. It looks serious."

He glanced down at his side, then ran a finger lightly over the wound and winced. "It is nothing more than a scratch. Do not worry yourself."

"Nonsense," Hattie said. "The least I can do is clean it for you. After all, you saved my life. I owe you something." She hurried into the tent and grabbed a pitcher of clean water and a linen towel. Dashing outside, she directed him to sit on the stool, which she hastily righted.

"I do not need assistance, Hattie," he protested as she pushed him down.

"Please, Senemut," she said. "I stood by, helpless, and watched the battle below, and I watched your battle with the Nubian soldier. This is something that I can do. It will make me feel useful."

Senemut sighed. "Very well."

Hattie knelt next to him, dipped the towel in the water and dabbed it over the cut, removing the blood and dirt as gently as possible. She tried to ignore the tingles she felt when she ran her fingers over his chest and ribs, probing delicately for other hidden injuries.

"Hattie, I…" He stopped, swallowed, and started again. "Are you certain you are trained for this?"

"Am I hurting you?" she murmured, looking up into his eyes. "I am sorry. I am being as gentle as I can. Fortunately, the gash is not deep, and I think it is your only injury."

"Aye, and did I not tell you as much?" Senemut said, wincing, but returning her warm gaze. "Nonetheless, I thank you for your kindness."

"It was my pleasure." Hattie smiled. "There! It is finished. Try to keep it clean, and it will heal well."

Snefru suddenly appeared at her side, panting and covered with sweat and blood. His eyes widened as he noticed Senemut's injury, Hattie kneeling at his side with a bloody towel in her hand. When Hattie stood and faced him, he dragged his gaze away. "Majesty!" he cried, bowing. "A most glorious victory!"

"Aye." She bit her tongue to keep from telling him her true thoughts. "You did an excellent job, General Snefru. My congratulations."

"It is my pleasure to serve Your Majesty." He gestured at the battlefield. "We lost only seventy men, and two hundred are wounded. The enemy lost far more men."

"No doubt," she murmured. "There is one." She pointed at the downed Nubian soldier, still lying unconscious and covered with pottery fragments. "He tried to kill me, but Lord Senemut saved my life. How did he slip past your soldiers?"

"I…I swear, I know not, Majesty!" Snefru stammered, bowing low. "But all things are possible in battle. Senemut, Egypt owes you…owes you a great debt." He glared at Senemut with a less than kindly expression on his face. "I will have this Nubian dog dragged from your sight at once, Royal One," he continued, prodding the warrior with a foot. "We have captured the leader of the traitors. Shall I have him brought to your tent?"

She glanced down at the field, where the dead were being dragged away and the wounded tended. "Nay. Hold him for the present. I wish to see to the needs of the wounded."

"But, Majesty, the physicians are quite capable of—"

"Mayhap so. But my soldiers were wounded in my service, and I wish to assure myself they are properly treated. Thank you, General Snefru." She dismissed him with a curt wave.

He bowed again and hastened away.

She turned to Senemut. "You need not accompany me if you choose not to. But it is something I must do."

He grinned. "It is my honor to follow you onto the field of battle, or anywhere else you desire to go, little warrior. And it may be that you will need my protection again! Or mayhap I will need yours. Have you other wine jars?" he asked, winking. Then he reached for her hand.

So, with Senemut at her side, Hattie moved among the wounded lying on the field, assisting the physicians in removing arrows, stitching wounds, applying bandages, setting broken limbs, and comforting the dying.

Hours passed, and the sun had nearly set before she straightened painfully and trudged slowly up the hill to her tent. She was covered with blood and dirt, and much of her gown she had torn away to use as bandages. Fatigue hung heavy on her like a shroud. She felt she had aged an eternity in the last twenty-four hours.

She slumped down on a stool inside the tent. Senemut stood in front of her. "You are tired, are you not, little warrior?"

"Aye," she murmured. "So tired. I have pains in muscles I did not know I possessed."

"May I assist you with that?" he asked. "You cared for me. I would be honored to do as much for you."

"Of course. What did you have in mind?"

Senemut rose and stepped behind her. She felt his warm, strong hands on her shoulders, tentatively at first. Then, with more assurance, he firmly massaged her aching muscles. Hattie relaxed, giving in to the sensuous pleasure of his hands on her flesh.

"You were wonderful, Hattie," he said as he kneaded the sore muscles in her back. "Your name will live forever in your soldiers' hearts."

"I do not feel wonderful," she mumbled. "I feel dirty, inside and out. I am exhausted."

"Ah! This, I can remedy." He clapped his hands, and an orderly rushed into the tent. "Bring Her Majesty's bath."

"At once, Your Lordship."

The orderly rushed away, returning quickly with a collapsible canvas tub. Several men followed, carrying large stone jars of water, which they poured into the tub. Then they vanished as quickly as they had come, closing the tent flaps behind them.

"Oh, Senemut." Hattie eyed the water greedily. "I would love a bath. But I am so tired, I fear I cannot manage."

"Then, allow me, Majesty. It would be my pleasure to assist you."

Gasping, she raised her gaze to his. Love shone from every line of his face as he reached out a hand to her.

"Aye," she whispered, taking his hand. "Aye, Senemut."

He pulled her gently to her feet. "First, we must remove what remains of your poor gown," he said as he swiftly and efficiently unfastened it, allowing the ragged linen to drop to the floor at her feet.

She stood silent, holding her head high, though her cheeks flamed with color. She heard the sharp intake of his breath as his gaze swept over her body.

"By Amun, you are the most beautiful woman I have ever seen," he breathed.

He scooped her up into his arms, and at that point, she was ready to go with him wherever he chose to take her. But instead of her bed, he deposited her gently in the tub.

The water was lukewarm and blissfully clean. She closed her eyes as Senemut poured dipper after dipper of water over her head. Then, he slowly massaged her hair and body with his strong, sensitive hands. A comforting, numbing heat flooded through her like strong wine.

At last he pulled her to an upright position and helped her out of the tub, then gently stroked her body dry with linen towels.

Hattie could scarcely keep her eyes open as he lifted her again into his arms and carried her to the bed.

"I am sorry, Senemut," she mumbled, trying to keep her eyes open. "You deserve more, but I am so tired."

He pulled the sheet up over her and smoothed her hair off her forehead, then lay down on the floor next to her bed. "Sleep, little one," he murmured, his voice low and soothing. "I am here to keep you safe. Sleep."

Hattie sighed, curled up and dropped quickly into merciful slumber.

* * *

Senemut tossed and turned on the hard floor beside Hattie's bed. She had been asleep for hours, but he lay wide awake. Her delicate fragrance drifted down to him as the gentle sound of her breathing enveloped him. He groaned. Hori was right—he was helplessly in love with her. How had it happened? Hatshepsut had never meant more to Senemut than any other member of the royal family— someone to command his actions, not his heart. But since her husband's death, she had changed. She was more decisive, more forthright, more sure of herself. It made her a better ruler. It also made her exceedingly seductive.

He turned over and sighed. Regardless of how alluring she was, Hatshepsut was the regent and ruler of all Egypt, and he was but a common-born man. She had elevated him to a position of great authority, and she relied on his advice. Both were great honors, greater than he dared hope. But that in no way implied she desired his love. And even if she did… Senemut held his head in his hands. That way lay madness. For surely, to consummate such a love was to risk the wrath of all Egypt, and beyond that, the wrath of the gods.

A faint sound roused him from his feverish thoughts. Frowning, he rose swiftly, ready to face whatever enemy appeared. The sound came again. It was Hattie, moaning in her sleep, harsh lines of fear etched into her face. "Nay," she groaned, tossing and turning. "Please, do not…"

"Shh, little one," Senemut whispered, bending over her and

stroking her hair. "Sleep, now. All is well." He watched her face relax. She sighed, then turned over and fell again into a deep sleep.

Caressing her hair one last time, he stared down at her now-peaceful face. His heart contracted painfully. Great Amun, how could he endure one more hour without folding her slender body in his arms, kissing her irresistible lips, professing his eternal love? Yet, how could he do any of those things and live? Clenching his jaw, he moved quietly away from the bed. It was almost dawn, and the camp would be stirring soon. For both their sakes, it was best that no one find him sleeping next to Hatshepsut's bed.

CHAPTER 12

Hattie awakened the next morning stiff and sore, but strangely at peace. She opened her eyes slowly. Senemut was gone. She seemed to remember him whispering something about keeping watch outside once the sun rose.

The bathtub was still in place. She arose from the bed and splashed some water on her face, then reached into a trunk for a fresh gown. She was struggling to fasten it when Senemut entered without ceremony.

He took in the scene at a glance and strode to her side. "Let me help you, Hattie." Swiftly, he fastened the gown over her left shoulder. "Did you sleep well?"

"Aye, I did." Hattie blushed. "Thank you for your help last night, and for saving my life. I fear I gave you poor recompense."

Senemut reached out and touched her cheek lightly with his fingertips. "You were most merciful on the battlefield yesterday. Your soldiers can speak of nothing else."

"It was certainly the least I could do, considering I sent them into the slaughter," she mumbled.

"Aye, well, that is the nature of battle." He shrugged. "Are you ready? Snefru has been holding the leader of the Nubians, as you requested. Will you sentence him now?"

Hattie sighed. "Aye. Of course. Bring him to my tent."

Senemut left, and shortly returned. Snefru followed close at his heels, dragging a nearly naked Nubian warrior behind him, trussed up in shackles like a runaway slave.

"Majesty…" Snefru cuffed the prisoner and forced him to his knees. "This…this *jackal* is the leader of the rebels. What is

Your Majesty's pleasure? Shall I have the royal archers put him to death? Or mayhap Your Majesty would like to return him home to Egypt, and hang him by his heels outside the palace walls for all to see what becomes of those who rise up against pharaoh."

"Be silent." She waved her hand at Snefru, and then turned her attention to the prisoner. "You, there, what is your name?"

The man raised his head. Bruises covered his dark face; one eye had swollen almost shut. Cuts and scrapes covered his muscular torso, and a long gash ran the length of one forearm. Obviously, he had personally led his soldiers into combat. She saw fear shining from his eyes, but also a great deal of pride. He clenched his jaw tightly shut and said nothing, flexing his strong arms against the chains that bound him.

"Remove his chains," she ordered quietly.

"But, Majesty—" Snefru began. She cut him short with a glance and he hastened to do her bidding, though he threw more than one critical look over his shoulder. As soon as he was free, the Nubian rose to his feet and massaged his chafed wrists. He did not respond to Hattie's question.

"Come, now. I will see you come to no harm. What is the danger in telling me your name?"

He raised his eyes to hers briefly. "My name is Piye, Royal One. I am chief of the Nubian bowmen, and commander of the army."

"Thank you, Piye. I am Hatshepsut, queen regent of Egypt. Do you know that your country is a vassal state of Egypt, and bound to obey her rule?"

"Aye, Royal One," he ground out from between clenched teeth. "We are your slaves and your property."

"Nonsense. You are under the protection of Egypt—an arrangement that can be mutually beneficial."

"It has not been so thus far," he muttered, shaking his head.

"Then we will have to change that." She clapped her hands for her scribe.

"What does Your Majesty have in mind?" Snefru asked, suspicion evident in his narrowed eyes.

Hattie beckoned the scribe to take a seat. "I will offer a treaty to the Nubians. They will remain loyal subjects, in return for which, I will promise them trading and other benefits."

This was too much for Snefru to stomach. "But, Majesty!" he cried. "They are Egypt's vassals! You need not promise them anything. It is their duty to obey."

Senemut leaned down and whispered in her ear. "I fear Snefru is right. If you treat them kindly, they will take advantage of it. You must be firm."

"I intend to be firm," she retorted. "But I also intend to be fair. I would rather have Nubia as my ally than my enemy. A friend will guard you from assault, but an enemy will stab you in the back."

Senemut shook his head, but subsided into silence. Piye glanced at her, surprise written across his strong features.

"I will ask you to sign this papyrus, Piye, promising that you and your people will be loyal subjects of Egypt. You will obey our laws, and send your annual tribute as required. You will not rebel against us. Your signature will be your sacred oath." She held up her hand to stop the prisoner from speaking. "In return, I will promise you that none of your countrymen will be harmed if they obey our laws. Egypt will trade frequently with your country. In addition, we will send soldiers to your assistance if it is required, just as you will assist us when necessary. Do you agree?"

Piye's jaw dropped. "Royal One, I…I know not what to say. Forgive me, but pharaohs have never dealt with us thus."

"You have never dealt with me before. Come, give me your answer—will you be Egypt's enemy or Egypt's ally?" Hattie stared at him, chin held high.

"Ally, Royal One," the man at last responded in a whisper. "Ally! I will serve Your Majesty until the day I die."

* * *

Hapuseneb stared at Snefru in openmouthed horror. "He what?"

"Aye, you heard me aright," Snefru said bitterly. "That commoner Senemut saved Hatshepsut's life, dispatching the Nubian soldier who was directed to kill her. And Senemut received barely a scratch in the process."

"*Ast!* Senemut should be dragged into the desert and left to die!

He is a scourge upon Egypt." Hapuseneb slumped heavily onto a stool. "And that woman must be protected by Horus himself."

"Horus or no, we must do something before she brings Egypt down…and us with it." Snefru glared at Hapuseneb. "Not only did Senemut save her life, but somehow—I know not through what magic or spell—he convinced her to offer a treaty to the Nubians instead of punishing them as they deserve."

"A treaty?" Hapuseneb's stomach plunged sickeningly. His beloved Egypt would be brought to ruin in Hatshepsut's foolish hands. "What will become of Egypt under the rule of that woman? With Senemut at her side, she will destroy us all, leaving Egypt's bones to be picked over by the scavengers. We must stop her!"

"Aye, we must. Have you other ideas?"

"Give me time, give me time…" Hapuseneb steepled his hands and tapped his index fingers together. Then the glimmering of an idea appeared in his desperately searching mind. It was preposterous, but it just might work. "Aye! I have it! I know how we will bring her down. It is risky, but it will work—it must! Here is what we will do…"

Snefru leaned his dark head close to Hapuseneb's shaved one, and they murmured together until dawn broke in the eastern sky.

CHAPTER 13

Hattie sighed as Tuthmosis fled the throne room, his tears barely held in check. General Snefru followed close on his heels, furious, but better able to contain his emotions after years spent in pharaoh's service.

Hattie turned to Senemut. "Was I wrong?"

His face was carefully neutral. "It is not my place, Majesty, to instruct you in—"

"*Ast!*" she snapped. "I asked for your opinion, did I not?"

"Aye. I am sorry, Hattie." He bowed briefly. "It is…it is *customary* for young princes to accompany their armies on campaigns. It is natural that His Majesty Prince Tuthmosis would wish to do so. It is considered part of a royal prince's education, and the experience will be very valuable for him when he mounts the throne."

"I know, I know," Hattie agreed impatiently. "But he is only eight years old. He is a baby! Surely, he is too young to go off to war, despite all his protests to the contrary."

"Many have gone at a younger age, Majesty," Senemut murmured. "He would have countless advisors and guards around him, and General Snefru would see to it that he came to no harm. A boy his age is ready to learn about discipline and command, which are abilities he will surely need when he rules Egypt."

"Aye, well, I will consider it. But I do not think I will change my mind. I have seen battle now, and it is a hideous, terrifying thing." Her frown softened. "Tuthmosis is only a child and does not know what is best for him. Sometimes I must go against his wishes, causing him to fear and distrust me more. Nothing I do pleases him, and I have tried very hard to please him for the past six months. He is a sad little boy with a great weight on his shoulders, but he will not allow me to help him."

"He is young, as you said. Give him time. He still mourns the loss of his father, and chafes under the restrictions of being a ruler with no real authority. He will come around, I am certain."

"Mayhap you are right. But I grow weary of trying to impress an unresponsive boy, regardless of the reasons for his stubbornness. I feel strongly about this issue, and I do not think I will change my mind." Hattie sighed again. "Tell General Snefru he may proceed with the campaign, *without* Prince Tuthmosis."

"Very well, Majesty. It shall be as you command." Senemut bowed and left the room.

"Campaigns," Hattie muttered as she stormed back to her royal suite. Servants in the halls bowed submissively and shrank before her wrath. "Soldiers. Little boys running off to make war! I am sick of it all. I want to go home to my own time, my own country, my own friends. I cannot stand this exile a moment longer." She marched into her bedroom, tore the coronet from her head, and flung it onto the bed.

Nesi awaited her, a look of abject fear etched across her face. "May I serve you, Majesty?" she whispered.

"Bring me some food, and be quick about it," Hattie snapped.

"Aye, Majesty." Nesi turned to go, quaking so violently that her fragile gown shivered with each step.

At once, Hattie's conscience stabbed her. "Nesi?"

"Aye, Majesty?" The servant turned with obvious reluctance to face her mistress again.

"I am sorry I shouted at you. I am not angry with you. Please accept my apology," Hattie said in a warmer tone. She smiled encouragingly.

Nesi blushed. "It is nothing. I am but Your Majesty's servant."

"And you deserve to be treated fairly. You have been a great help to me, and I value your service."

"Thank you, Majesty." Nesi curtseyed deeply. "I am honored I have been of use to Your Royal Highness." The girl still appeared ill at ease, but at least her shaking had stopped.

"Please fetch me some date wine, a little cheese, and figs. And some bread, too, but take care that you bring bread made with the special flour. I do not wish to break a tooth."

The servant curtseyed once more and fled the room as if demons were chasing her.

Hattie was rather proud of herself for finding a way to insure she could eat bread without wearing her teeth down to a pulp on sandy grit. She had instructed the royal goldsmith in the preparation of a golden sieve covered with very fine holes, pierced with a tiny, sharp awl. She demonstrated to her astonished cook the use of the sieve, to strain out sand and other impurities from the flour. The cook was suitably impressed, too, with the delicacy of the finished baked goods. If only her other problems were so easy to solve!

Her refusal to allow Tuthmosis to accompany him on the army's next campaign had infuriated General Snefru. He had been most vocal in his support of the idea—dangerously close to insolent, in fact. Hattie knew so little about the time in which she found herself. Perhaps she should have allowed Tuthmosis to go. Senemut felt it was appropriate, after all, and she trusted him. Had she erred again? Perhaps the real Hatshepsut would have allowed Tuthmosis to train with the army. Was she jeopardizing her chances of returning home by forbidding the prince to go? She was charged with protecting him, but was she being overprotective?

Hattie dropped down onto her bed and pressed her fingers against her aching temples. What she wouldn't give for a couple of aspirins! She needed to concentrate on finding a way back home where she wouldn't have to worry about campaigns, sulky crown princes, or damaging her teeth in a place where the practice of dentistry was limited to chanting a prayer to ward off evil, and wrenching the offending tooth out of the inebriated patient's jaw.

Traveling through time was easier said than done, however. Hattie still didn't know for certain how she had ended up in Hatshepsut's court, so she didn't have the first idea of how to return home, although she strongly suspected the necklace had something to do with it. Her memory continued to be a bit hazy, most probably from the blow to the head she'd sustained when she fell in the vault at the museum. The last thing she remembered was a wave of dizziness, clutching the necklace, and falling to the floor, then a brief, dreamlike encounter with the image of Hatshepsut. When she awoke, she discovered she had been given—without her permission—a splitting headache, a different body, a new life, and an apparently one-way ticket to the past.

Tuthmosis was not making that new life any easier. Every time she tried to reach out to the boy to befriend him, he ignored her or turned away. He still seemed to be struggling with the loss of his father and the adult responsibilities suddenly thrust upon him. Yet he wouldn't accept help from Hattie, the one person who wanted to ease his pain.

Senemut had suggested, when she first arrived, that the boy be sent away to train with the army. And now it was clear General Snefru agreed. She had rejected the advice out of hand, thinking Tuthmosis was too young, but perhaps she had been hasty in reaching that conclusion. Boys in her own time, often as young as Tuthmosis, went to military academies. It was a good way to instill discipline and a healthy respect for authority. Perhaps sending Tuthmosis into the army was the ancient world's equivalent of military school?

She would discuss it with Senemut the next time she saw him. He might have been right all along. He was a native in this time, after all, while she was just an interloper. She should give his advice more credence.

The curtain flew to one side and a tiny figure burst into the room. "Mother!" Neferure ran to Hattie and threw her small arms around Hattie's knees, effectively pinning her in place.

"Hello, darling." Hattie gently disengaged the child and lifted her into her arms. "I am happy to see you, but should you not be at your lessons?"

"I wanted to see you. Senimen will not mind." Neferure flung her arms around Hattie's neck.

Hattie patted the girl's back and bounced her up and down as she walked across the room. "Do you like your new tutor?" she asked, setting Neferure down on the bed.

"Aye, Mother, I like him well enough. But why do you not teach me?"

"I am sorry, little one, but I have too many other duties. Senimen will teach you well, if you mind him."

"I shall." Neferure nodded emphatically. "I am a very good girl. Senimen says so."

Hattie heard a cough outside her door. "Come in."

Senimen poked his dark head into the room. "Ah, there you are, Princess Neferure! You must not run away from me at lesson time." He sketched a brief bow to Hattie. "Forgive the intrusion, Your Majesty. I shall see it does not happen again."

Hattie chuckled. "Never mind, Senimen. I enjoy seeing Neferure and hearing of her progress." She turned to the child. "Back to your lessons, little one. Off you go! There are many things you must learn so that, when you grow up, you can be a good queen."

She sighed as she watched Neferure's sturdy little legs carry her down the hall in the direction of her own rooms, hand-in-hand with Senimen. Hattie had grown very fond of the little princess, and it was becoming increasingly difficult to imagine leaving her behind when she returned to her own time. Well, who wouldn't be fond of such a pretty, intelligent and affectionate child? It wasn't Neferure's fault that the woman she thought to be her mother was really an intruder from another place and time. It was Hattie's duty to treat the child as Hatshepsut would. Neferure didn't deserve to suffer for Hattie's misfortune, regardless of how it would break Hattie's heart to leave her when the time came.

The curtain flapped again. "Neferure, I thought I told you to…" Hattie began. But it was Senemut striding into her room, not the child. His expression was grim. "What is it?" she asked. "Did the prince throw another temper tantrum?"

"Nay, Majesty. But it does concern the prince. I have something to tell you that I fear will alarm you. It is most serious."

Her knees buckled and she sat down abruptly on the bed. "What is it? Tell me." Filled with a sudden, dark foreboding, she held her breath, waiting for his response.

He hesitated, then boldly took both of Hattie's hands in his and squeezed them tightly. "Hattie, someone has tried to murder Prince Tuthmosis."

CHAPTER 14

"Someone tried to kill Tuthmosis?" Hattie gasped. "Who? How? Is he all right? Tell me what happened, Senemut."

"He is all right," Senemut assured her, sitting down next to her on the bed. "He is just a little frightened. I have had him taken to my rooms, and placed under the protection of my own bodyguards. He is safe...at least for now."

Hattie passed a shaky hand across her brow. "How did this happen? Tell me quickly, Senemut. Who would want to harm that little boy?"

He frowned. "There are many who would wish to harm a crown prince and heir to the throne. It is a miracle when any royal child reaches maturity."

"What happened?" she repeated impatiently.

"Tuthmosis was about to have a meal. One of the ladies of the royal harem brought him his favorite food—barley porridge and honey cakes."

Hattie nodded. She knew the boy had a sweet tooth, and had tried to win him over with honey cakes herself on more than one occasion.

"His tutor, Ineni, told the prince that he must eat his porridge before he could have his honey cakes," Senemut continued. "While Tuthmosis was eating the porridge, his pet monkey stole one of the cakes and ran off with it. Within five minutes, the monkey was dead."

She gasped. "Poison?"

"Aye. A virulent, quick-acting poison. Had Tuthmosis eaten the honey cake himself, he would most probably be dead."

79

Hattie leapt up and paced the floor. "Who would want to harm him? He is just a little boy. Even if he is the crown prince, surely he poses no danger to anyone at his age? He pays little enough attention in court. For all the input he provides, I might as well be making the decisions alone."

The expression on Senemut's face was strained. "Hattie, I do not think…I do not think the honey cakes were poisoned because Tuthmosis was a threat to anyone. I very much fear the poisoner was attempting to get rid of *you*."

"Me?" she cried. "Why would anyone want to get rid of me? And why would they poison Tuthmosis to do it? If he had eaten the poisoned sweet and died, I would still be here to…to rule."

Senemut slowly shook his head. "If the crown prince were to die, you would no longer be Regent on the throne of Egypt. You are a woman, and cannot rule alone. By getting rid of Tuthmosis, a traitor could rid himself of both of you."

Hattie twisted her hands together. "But, if someone wants to get rid of me, why did he not try to poison me? Why Tuthmosis? Surely, it would be simpler to just kill me."

Senemut sighed. "I, too, have pondered this and I will tell you my thoughts, though they may be incorrect. As Regent, you are too well guarded to make an attempt on your life easy. You are not as impulsive as a child. The traitor would have to come up with something less transparent than poisoning an item of food you did not request."

He hesitated, then continued. "Yet it may be the traitor has already tried to rid himself of you also. I thought you had died of grief at your husband, the Great God's funeral, but it may be that you, too, were poisoned and the assassin simply misjudged the strength of the poison. May Amun forgive me, but I believe it makes sense for him to use the same means to murder both you and Tuthmosis."

Nausea crawled around in the pit of Hattie's stomach. She'd thought her worries were confined to dealing with recalcitrant princes and finding her way back home. She had forgotten the warning of the real Hatshepsut that the would-be assassin might have already tried to kill her once; she hadn't believed her own life might be in danger. "Who did it? Who put the poison in the honey cake?"

Again, he shook his head. "I know not. The woman who brought the food is being questioned, but I fear we will learn nothing from her. The food was given to her by a servant, who, in turn, received it from one of the royal cooks. That cook has since disappeared."

"Well, find him!" she cried. "We must find out who did this, and have the traitor imprisoned. Then, the prince will be safe." *And so will I*, she added silently.

"The guards are searching for the cook and questioning the other servants, but I fear the unfortunate servant was not the originator of the plot. He was no doubt a pawn in a much larger scheme."

"But he could tell us who is to blame," she insisted. "We must find him."

Senemut sighed and shook his head. "I fear if we do find him, it will be at the bottom of the Nile."

Of course. A fiend who wouldn't hesitate to murder a small boy would have no qualms about getting rid of a servant who could point the finger of blame at him. "What shall we do then, Senemut? How can we protect Tuthmosis? Surely, they will try again."

"I fear you are right, Hattie. And the boy may not be so lucky the next time. We must find a way to protect him. It is difficult when we know not whom to trust." Senemut pursed his lips in thought.

Hattie, too, puzzled over the situation. She struggled to recall what little she knew of the life of the real Hatshepsut. Perhaps something in that history could help her now. But, try as she might, she couldn't remember any mention of an assassination attempt on Prince Tuthmosis. Most of what she knew concerned the coronation ceremony when Hatshepsut was crowned pharaoh, although she did remember that Tuthmosis finally came to the throne after Hatshepsut had ruled for a number of years. From that, it appeared Tuthmosis was not the target of any assassination attempts. Or, at least, he survived them to rule after Hatshepsut.

Pharaoh...wait a minute. Hattie was simply serving as regent for Tuthmosis. No coronation had taken place. Yet, history told her that Hatshepsut had ruled alone, as Pharaoh of all Egypt. What would happen if Hattie were to be crowned now? Would it change the situation? Would it protect the prince?

One thing was certain: if she were pharaoh, there would be no sense in assassinating Tuthmosis. Hattie herself would be the only one in danger. And though the traitor was obviously bold, he might not dare lift his hand against pharaoh himself. *Herself*, Hattie amended. It was a bold plan, but it was worth a try.

"Senemut, I think I have the answer, but you may not like it. Will you hear me out?"

He looked up at her. "I would be glad to listen to any idea of how we can protect the prince."

"In order to protect Tuthmosis, we must find a way..." She paused to gather her thoughts. "We must find some way to have me proclaimed pharaoh. Then there would be no point in further attempts on Tuthmosis's life and he would be spared. Is that not so?" She clenched her hands in tense fists, waiting to hear his reaction to her startling proposal.

Senemut's jaw dropped. "Pharaoh? But...but...you are a woman!"

She smiled. "I am glad you have noticed."

"Nay, nay, that is not what I mean," he stammered. "Pharaoh must be a man! He is the living incarnation of Horus, and he rules over all Egypt. He is ruler...judge...warrior...defender. He must be male."

Hattie realized she was asking a lot of Senemut. There were many men in the twenty-first century who had difficulty with the concept of women's equality, and Senemut hadn't had the benefit of nearly thirty-five hundred years of gradual emancipation to get used to the idea.

"Have I not been ruler of all Egypt these past months?" she asked gently. "Did I not lead my troops into battle? Have I not built a peaceful relationship with Nubia? Do you think a man would have done better?"

Senemut swallowed. He might not be a modern man, but Hattie

knew he was honest. "Nay, Hattie. A man might have handled the situation differently, but I do not believe he could have produced a better outcome. And I confess, I find your judgment sound."

"This is the only way we can safeguard the boy," she continued. "If I were pharaoh, his life would no longer be in danger. There would be no point in killing him because it would have no effect on me. I would still rule Egypt."

"But *you* would still be in danger with this plan of yours. Far greater danger, mayhap," he protested, his face stricken.

She shrugged. "I am in danger now. But I think this traitor is a coward. He chooses to work through poison and intrigue, instead of open confrontation. He surely will not dare try to murder pharaoh."

"Possibly, but mayhap he would." Scowling, Senemut paced back and forth, his hands clasped behind his back.

Hattie could tell he was torn between the logic of her arguments, and the centuries of Egyptian tradition. It was a tribute to his great intelligence and open-mindedness that he would even consider her proposal.

At last, he turned to her with a strange expression on his face. She watched him carefully, waiting to hear his answer. Two lives depended on it—the young prince's, and hers.

Dropping down on one knee, he placed his right hand over his heart. He locked his gaze with hers and said solemnly, "I pledge my loyalty and my life to you, Hatshepsut, incarnation of the living Horus, Pharaoh of all Egypt."

CHAPTER 15

Hattie swallowed hard, trying to force back the tears that sprang to her eyes. "Thank you, Senemut. I cannot accomplish this without your help." She grasped his hands and pulled him to his feet. "What must we do now?"

Senemut resumed pacing, his hands clasped behind his back. "First, all work on your mortuary temple in the Valley of the Queens must cease."

Mortuary temple? Hattie was not aware such a structure was under construction in her name, although she knew it was common practice among royalty to build for themselves magnificent tombs and temples, known as "houses for eternity". "Why must the construction on my mortuary temple cease? What does this have to do with having me named pharaoh?"

"You will no longer be a queen. You will be pharaoh…you will be king. Therefore, we will begin construction of a new tomb for you in the Valley of the Kings, as befits your new rank, and a magnificent mortuary temple. Mayhap your temple should be…" He paused a moment. "I have it! We shall build your temple on the west bank of the Nile. There is a perfect spot next to the ancient temple of Pharaoh Mentuhotep II. That spot is sacred to Hathor, goddess of love and music."

Hattie nodded enthusiastically. "I like it!" Closing her eyes, she pictured Hatshepsut's temple from photos she'd seen in the books Tom had pressed on her. "Can we have terraces and white-pillared colonnades?"

Senemut's eyes widened. "Little one, you have the soul of an artist. Aye, I can see it in my mind. The terraces must rise until

84

they meet the cliffs. I vow it will be the most splendid temple the world has known and, with Your Majesty's permission, I will design it thus."

Of course! Hattie had forgotten that one of his titles, in those same books, was Royal Architect. "Aye, Senemut! Please do design it. I know it will be exquisite under your direction. What else?"

"We must begin work at once," Senemut explained. "The walls of your new temple will be covered with reliefs illustrating your divine conception and birth." His brow furrowed in thought. "We must show you visiting shrines of the gods, accompanied by your father Tuthmosis I, and scenes of your coronation before the gods and here on earth. We will illustrate your father presenting you to the court, and formally nominating you as his co-regent and intended successor."

"But...but he did not do that. Did he?" Hattie asked.

Senemut frowned at her. "You must never speak thus. If we are to succeed in having you crowned pharaoh, there must be no doubt that you are the chosen one, both by your royal father and by the gods. It is the only way you will be accepted. From this day forth, on every monument, each document, and in every public utterance, you will be referred to as 'he' or 'His Majesty'."

"But, surely the people will know that it is not true," she protested. "They will know that my...my father did not name me his successor. And they can see I am a woman! Can I not be proclaimed pharaoh by virtue of my heritage, my intelligence, and my ability to handle the responsibilities of ruler?"

"Nay. The people will not accept you thus." Senemut touched her cheek briefly. "They will not know whether your royal father chose you as his successor or not. They are not privy to court affairs. And though you wear the outward guise of a woman, they must believe you have the spirit, the fierceness, of a man. Do not fear...they will believe."

"What about the nobles and the priests? Surely they, at least, will know the truth."

"The gods themselves have named you pharaoh. That is how it *must* be. In time, the nobles and priests, too, will come to believe it. They will forget that it was not ever thus. And you must never say otherwise," he warned. "They must be afraid to dispute your word, and that of the gods."

It's a little like the massive publicity campaigns launched by politicians in my time, Hattie thought—except that here, the propaganda would come *after* her succession to the post, not before. "What else?"

"You will not like this. You must honor your earthly father in every way possible, and you must ignore the memory of your husband. It is necessary for you to be identified with your father in order to justify your claim to the throne," Senemut said. "We will redesign your father's tomb in the Valley of the Kings and build him a new mortuary chapel associated with your own."

Hattie winced. "I do not wish to ignore the memory of my… of Neferure's father. It will hurt her to do so. And if I act thus, young Tuthmosis will never forgive me."

"Nevertheless, you must do so," he said harshly. "It is the only way. If we are to make you pharaoh, you must be willing to make these sacrifices. Are you willing? If you are not, then we must cease this speculation now, and think of another way to protect the boy, though I know not what." He paused, watching her face carefully.

Hattie was torn. She would pluck her own heart out before she would hurt little Neferure. And she had no wish to alienate Tuthmosis even further; their relationship was strained enough as it was. Yet she had to assure his safety. How ironic that the best way to protect his life was to further estrange him from her.

She sighed and squared her shoulders. "I will do what must be done, Senemut. Amun help me, I wish there were another way, but I fear there is not. I will not shrink from my duty."

His sudden smile was like a burst of sunshine from behind a storm cloud. "You are brave, little one," he murmured. "You certainly have the heart of a pharaoh."

Hattie's heart leapt at his praise. "Thank you, Senemut. But I could not accomplish it without you."

"Your Majesty is gracious," he said, bowing deeply to her. He arose with a twinkle in his eyes. "Now, we must choose your throne name. What shall it be?"

"What is wrong with Hatshepsut?" she demanded.

"Of course, that is your name," he said soothingly. "But your throne name must link you with the gods. It must show that you are divine and are suited to rule over Egypt, vanquishing all who dare oppose you."

Hattie whistled. "It will have to be quite a name to accomplish all that. Do you have any suggestions?"

"Let me think." He paused for a moment. "Aye, I think I have it! We shall call you, 'Powerful of Kas, flourishing of years, divine of diadems, Maatkare, Khenmet-Amun Hatshepsut'. What think you of it?" He grinned at her.

"I think it is quite a mouthful," she retorted. "How can anyone address me using that name? It will take them an afternoon simply to say it."

"It is merely your throne name, Hattie," Senemut scolded her gently. "No one will call you that. They may refer to you as Maatkare, or they will use your own name." He lifted an eyebrow. "And what shall I call you, Majesty?"

"Hattie, please," she said at once. "I cannot bear it if you call me otherwise."

"Hattie it shall be then," he agreed. "In private. In public, you shall be my pharaoh and my king, His Majesty Maatkare, Ruler of the Two Lands!"

She gulped. If there was ever a time to awaken from this dream, to return to her own world and leave the past behind, now was that time. If this nightmare didn't end, if she couldn't find a way to return to her own life immediately, then she feared there was no turning back. Soon, Hattie Williams, an obscure artist from twenty-first century Chicago, would be sole ruler of all eighteenth dynasty Egypt.

CHAPTER 16

"Where are we going, Senemut?" Hattie asked for the fifth time.

For the fifth time, Senemut merely raised his eyebrows and said, "Have patience, little one."

Hattie grinned. There was no doubt about it—the man guarded a secret better than the sands of the desert. Whatever he had planned was bound to be marvelous. Trying to be patient, she leaned back and let the welcome breeze drift over her as the oarsmen dipped and pulled, taking them swiftly across the Nile to the west bank. Though the sun was just rising, the day was already hot.

They landed and Senemut helped her out of the boat.

"Well?" she demanded. "What is the surprise?"

"We walk now."

Sighing, Hattie gestured for him to lead the way, two guards trailing them at a respectful distance. He would tell her in his own good time.

Hurrying to keep up, she followed him as they crossed a broad plain, then scrambled up a steep and precarious path that was little more than a goat trail, leaving the guards puffing and muttering in their wake. Pausing at the top of the ridge to catch her breath, she panted, "I go no farther until you tell me where you are taking me."

Senemut smiled broadly and pointed down. "Look. It is your temple."

Hattie turned her head to follow his pointing finger and gasped. Backed up to an impressive bay of limestone cliffs, glowing in the rosy light of dawn, stood the partially completed expanse of her temple. Although much work remained to be done, it was an imposing, magnificent sight. A broad causeway led from the river across the valley to the temple. Three sphinxes flanked one side of the avenue, and workmen were hard at work on another of what was obviously a long line of the creatures. Two terraces were in place, with wide ramps leading up from one to another, and a third was under construction.

"Oh, Senemut," Hattie breathed. "It is lovely. You are doing a wonderful job." She had seen Hatshepsut's ruined temple in the museum's photographs, but nothing had prepared her for the breathtaking sight of it in person. "I see there is an easier path," she added, indicating the sphinx-lined avenue. "But I am pleased you brought me this way. What a magnificent view!"

"You are not angry that I kept our destination from you?"

"Oh, nay. It is a wonderful surprise." She smiled. "Tell me about it, please. How will it look when it is completed?"

"It will be the most imposing temple in all of Egypt! There, in the first court, will be a garden, depictions of the marshes of lower Egypt, and scenes of Your Majesty's great obelisks for the temple at Karnak under construction," he said, pointing. "The second court will illustrate to all who come the events surrounding your divine birth, and the great accomplishments of your reign."

"Of course, it is blank thus far," Hattie murmured.

"But not for long, little warrior." Senemut grinned. "The south end of the second level will host a chapel dedicated to Hathor, goddess of love and music, on whose sacred site your temple is built. The chapel will include pillars capped with representations of Hathor and a hypostyle hall. And on the north end of the second level will be a chapel dedicated to Anubis."

"The god of the dead?"

Senemut nodded. "The uppermost court will have statues of Your Gracious Majesty—" He bowed deeply. "—before each pillar. A peristyle court leads to the rock chapel dedicated to Amun. Also, we will construct chapels for you and your royal father." He spread his arms to indicate the entire complex. "You are pleased?"

"I am awestruck," she assured him. "How could I be anything but pleased with such a magnificent structure?"

"The work will not be completed for many seasons," Senemut said, sighing. "But even a half-finished temple should have a name. Have you anything in mind?"

"A name?" Hattie closed her eyes and frowned. Had she ever heard a name for Hatshepsut's temple? She wracked her brain but couldn't remember one. The pictures she'd seen simply called it Hatshepsut's temple. Aloud, she said, "I know not what to call it, but the name should reflect its purpose, should it not? The temple will be dedicated to several gods. It will list the accomplishments of my reign. Priests will perform sacred rites there. It will be holy ground."

"Aye. It will be the holiest of the holies," Senemut said, nodding. Then he opened his eyes wide. "Holiest of the holies…that is it, Hattie! We shall call it *Djeser Djeseru*. What think you?"

"I think it is perfect," Hattie said, relieved. The name was unfamiliar but felt, somehow, right. "Can we get closer? I would like to see the artists at work." She pointed to the scaffolding around the pillars on the middle terrace.

"Of course!" Senemut held out his hand to her. "The workmen will be most honored by your presence."

She took his hand and, together, they started down the steep path to the temple.

Senemut led her to the foot of the cliffs. They walked up the sphinx-lined avenue, skirting sweating laborers who pulled and strained against the ropes around a giant limestone block, inching it toward the wall of the temple under construction. Overseers shouted directions and encouragement; women scurried here and there, dispensing water, bread, fish and dates. Hattie breathed deeply. The air smelled of stone dust, mud, and dried fish, and heat already rose in ripples from the ground. Closer to the temple, Senemut pointed out T-shaped pits being excavated. "Those will be reflecting pools, surrounded by gardens," he explained.

He continued up the ramp to the court on the second level, Hattie close behind. There, a pair of colossal sphinxes was being carved out of red granite. "When the sculptors are finished, the sphinxes will be painted, as will those on the avenue," he said.

"They are magnificent," Hattie exclaimed, shading her eyes to look up to the top of the nearest one. She turned around in a circle. "And what is going on over there?" She pointed.

"The artisans are creating a series of reliefs illustrating Your Majesty's divine birth," Senemut said. "Would you like to examine their work?"

"Aye, I would!" She followed him to the nearest relief.

As soon as the workmen noticed Hattie, they fell to their knees, foreheads touching the dusty ground.

"Please rise," she urged. "I have come to see the splendid work you are doing." She walked over to a colorful, nearly completed relief of a pregnant woman in the company of two goddesses. "This is lovely! What does it represent?"

After a moment, a workman rose and approached her reluctantly, his gaze directed squarely at his feet. "Majesty, it is… it shows your royal mother, Queen Ahmose, being led into the birthing chamber by two goddesses who are there to witness your sacred birth."

Hattie asked, "And can you tell me how it is done? I am something of an artist myself, so I would like to know. The craftsmanship is exquisite."

The workman darted a glance up at her. She smiled encouragingly.

"First, Majesty, we chisel and smooth the rock walls," he said, pointing to another area of the temple where the walls were still rough and jagged. "Then, the wall must be coated with a thick layer of white plaster."

"I see," Hattie murmured. "What comes next?"

"An artist draws the subject onto the white plaster, Royal One. When he has finished, a master artist corrects and adds details to the drawing." He glanced up at her again and continued in a stronger voice, warming to his subject under her interested gaze. "Next, the sculptor chisels out the image, giving it depth and a lifelike effect. And finally, a master painter adds the colors and finishing touches."

"So it is a group effort, is it not?" Hattie asked.

The workman beamed. "Aye, Your Majesty, it is. We are honored to work on pharaoh's house of eternity, and we shall do our best to make it reflect your glory."

"You are doing a wonderful job," she said. "Please, do not let me interrupt your work any further. Thank you for educating me."

Blushing, the workman retreated, bowing low as he went.

Hattie turned to Senemut. "It is very striking! I had no idea it would be so…so overwhelming in scope and design. You are truly a talented architect, Senemut."

Senemut smiled. "It is my great honor and privilege to create a temple that befits Your Majesty in every way. As I said, it will take many seasons to complete." He looked around and dropped his voice. "Once you are crowned pharaoh on New Year's Day, you must begin your reign with a suitably impressive deed. Then the workmen can record it on the walls of your temple."

Hattie's stomach lurched and her smile faded. "Aye, I suppose you are right, though I know not what the impressive deed shall be." For a few minutes, she had forgotten the reason this temple was under construction—and it had been the most carefree time she'd had in a long while. But now, the burden of assuming the crown settled onto her again.

Senemut had done his work well over the past year. He'd had inscriptions carved, arranged for Hattie to make temple dedications and have her royal father's monuments restored, and lined up support of vassal states—with Nubia the first to fall in line, thanks to Hattie's fair treatment of them after their uprising. He'd spoken the correct words in the proper ears, and won over much of the priesthood and the army. Hattie was amazed at both his ingenuity and his tenacity. He'd refused to give up until he had garnered support for Hatshepsut's crowning from nearly every high official in the land.

Hapuseneb, the high priest of Amun, had selected New Year's Day as her coronation day. Unlike Hattie's images of New Year's Eve at Times Square, the Egyptian New Year began in late June, when the star they called Sopdet rose just above the horizon at dawn during the time of the annual flooding of the Nile.

At first, Hattie chafed under the delay until the next New Year's celebration. If she were forced to do the thing at all, she would prefer to get it over with quickly. But Senemut assured her it was both an auspicious and a practical choice, which allowed her regnal years and the civil calendar to coincide. "It is well," he had commented, "to begin your new life as pharaoh on the first day of a new year, when the Nile overflows and brings us her bounty. The gods will bless your reign."

Hattie wasn't so sure, but she didn't appear to have any choice in the matter. Once she'd suggested her accession to the throne would eliminate the threat against Tuthmosis, the decisions were removed from her hands. All she had to do was smile, follow Senemut's suggestions, and await the inexorable progression.

Suddenly, Hattie was no longer interested in watching the work progress on her temple. "I have a headache, Senemut," she whispered. "Please, take me home."

CHAPTER 17

Nesi came to prepare Hattie on the day of her coronation. Hattie was already awake, and had been tossing and turning since before dawn. "Come, Majesty. I have prepared your bath."

Hattie groaned. She had been dreading this day, and she wanted nothing more than to pull the sheet over her head and refuse to come out of her room until it was over. But time moved inescapably forward, and there was nothing she could do to stop its flow. Sighing, she arose and allowed Nesi to lead her into the bath chamber.

Before long, Nesi had worked her magic again. Hattie was dressed in a gossamer gown, gold and jewels around her neck and upper arms, and heavy rings on her fingers. Anointed with exotic perfumes, her hair dressed and face painted, she looked every inch the eighteenth dynasty Egyptian queen, and nothing like Hattie Williams from Chicago.

Hattie gulped and turned away from her reflection in the polished bronze mirror. What if she *never* returned to her own time? What if she were marooned here for the rest of her life? She had not been able to find the necklace, and had nearly given up looking for it. She'd spent hours poring over scrolls of magic incantations and charms, and had consulted—without revealing her true objective—priests and sorcerers, but to no avail. Her duties as Regent were now second nature to her, and she had adapted to the hardships of life in this era almost completely. Each day she became fonder and fonder of little Neferure, and even proud Prince Tuthmosis had wormed his way into her heart. And, though she was loath to admit it, each day she fell more deeply in love with Senemut. Would it be so bad, then, if she were to remain here?

I have to find a way to return home, she told herself with an impatient shake of her head. She firmly ignored the little voice in her heart that asked, *Why?*

Perhaps it was a mistake to continue to keep the truth from Senemut. His advice had always been sound, so might he not be able to advise her in this matter as well? Certainly, he knew more of the "magic" of the era—curses, magic spells and potions, amulets, love philters. Perhaps he knew of another way than the necklace to return her to her own time. Would he not want his own Hatshepsut back? Which Hatshepsut was he in love with?

The curtain to her bedchamber flew aside and Senemut strode into the room. Hattie's mouth dropped open as she stared at him. He was garbed in a finely pleated, white linen kilt with a wide gold sash, and woven leather sandals with curling tips. A broad gold collar surrounded his neck, and he wore wide gold armbands on his muscular upper arms. His eyes were accented by black kohl, and he wore an elaborately braided wig. The overall effect was exotic, alien, yet strangely compelling. He took her breath away.

She closed her mouth and shook herself. "Senemut, I have something to tell you—"

He crossed the room to her in three steps. "There is no time, Majesty. The ceremony is about to begin." He took her arm.

"But…" Hattie's heart lurched sickeningly, and her blood suddenly felt like ice coursing through her veins. "But I…"

"Later, Majesty. Amun—and Egypt—await you." He pulled her to the door.

Hattie breathed in short gasps, panic squeezing the air out of her lungs. She tried to concentrate on putting one foot in front of the other as Senemut led her out of the palace and to her chariot, waiting to take her to the temple. She'd never believed this day would actually come, so sure had she been that she'd return to her own time. What had she gotten herself into?

* * *

"She must have the gods on her side," Hapuseneb muttered,

jerking his priestly robes straight. "How else could she have raised enough support to see her—a woman—crowned pharaoh? I confess, I did not dream this day would come." He peered out again at the growing crowds surrounding the temple, and shook his head irritably.

"Pah! She has no gods to aid her," Snefru retorted. "She has Senemut. By Amun, he is far cleverer than I gave him credit for, especially when given free rein and an open purse. But never fear...I shall not underestimate him again."

"Aye. Senemut," the priest concurred. "He is like a thorn in our sides, always a step or two ahead of me. If only he would fall from her favor!" *Or if only he could be made to fall from her favor,* he silently added. *But how? He is wily and he neatly sidesteps every trap I set for him, from concubines to poison to assassins.*

"He will fall—in one fashion or another." Snefru smiled mirthlessly. "And once he is out of the way, our new 'pharaoh' will meet with an untimely accident, and be gathered to the gods. Such a pity...so young and so pretty. Tuthmosis will succeed her, but, of course, he is just a boy and must rely on his advisors."

"Aye—his High Priest of Amun, and his Great Army General." Hapuseneb grimaced. "I pray Amun it happens soon, else I might grow too impatient and make a mistake. We must be very careful now. We must not give ourselves away."

Snefru nodded. "You are wise, as always. So, go now and crown your new pharaoh. Give the ceremony all the pomp and gravity it deserves. Do nothing to draw unwanted attention to yourself! Do not fear—her reign will be brief."

* * *

The route to the temple of Amun in the sprawling Karnak temple complex was lined with cheering, shouting hordes. They jostled each other for a better view, hung from limbs of trees, and leaned precariously from rooftops of mud-brick houses and shops. Food vendors pushed through the crowd, hawking figs, dried fish, honey cakes, and beer. Parents balanced their children on their shoulders and pointed to Hattie as she passed. It wasn't every day the common folk were privileged to steal a glimpse of royalty.

Hattie was grateful for Senemut's advice that royalty did not smile, nor did they wave and gesture; they simply looked…regal. She knew she couldn't have held a smile in place on her frozen face, nor could she wave while clutching the side of the small gold and gem-encrusted chariot hard enough to leave impressions. The driver struggled mightily to control the two midnight-black horses that snorted, reared, and shied away from the jostling crowds, while Hattie feared the tiny chariot would overturn at any moment. She had no idea if the chariots of the royalty and nobles behind her in the procession were still following, or if they'd been delayed or upset by the crush of onlookers. She felt her wits had deserted her, and she prayed fiercely that she'd remember all of Senemut's instructions when the ceremony began.

At last, her chariot drew up in front of the temple of Amun in an impressive cloud of dust. There, Hapuseneb, the high priest of Amun, waited for her, along with scores of lesser priests. She sensed their dark, impassive gazes as she stepped down from the chariot and she felt suddenly, fiercely alone. Holding her head high and trying to remember to breathe instead of choking on the dust, she allowed Hapuseneb to lead her into the temple.

Senemut had told her that the first part of the coronation ceremony was the ritual purification. The strong, heady scent of incense tickled her nostrils as she entered the temple. Four priests, dressed and elaborately masked to represent the four gods Horus, Amun, Re, and Ptah, sprinkled her with water as they chanted blessings for her and her reign.

"Long live Horus, whose words are wise; whose counsels are astute; who brings the Two Lands into being. King of Upper and Lower Egypt, Lord of the Two Lands, Maatkare whom Re has chosen. Son of Re, Lord of Crowns, Hatshepsut beloved of Amun, beloved of Horus, may he have life eternal."

A droplet of cold water struck her in the face and she gasped. At once, she was reminded of the more familiar baptisms in her own time, complete with babies garbed in white, proud parents, and crowds of relatives. Her breath came a little easier. She felt more at ease and suppressed a smile.

"You must now take possession of your kingdom, Majesty," Hapuseneb muttered, snapping her out of her reverie.

Fortunately, Senemut had briefed Hattie on every aspect of the coronation, and she knew what she was to do next. She stalked out of the temple as majestically as she could, followed by Hapuseneb and the other priests. Gripping the crook and the flail, symbols of her royalty, she strode around the outer walls of the temple, pausing at each corner for prayers to be said, trying to project an aura of command and confidence. The crowd watched in absolute silence and stillness, as if they had become paintings on a tomb wall. The only sound was the whisper of her sandals in the dust. Then, a collective sigh of relief rippled through the group as she rounded the last corner and the last prayer was chanted.

"Scribe!" Hapuseneb motioned to a wizened old man lurking in the background, who hastened to his side with a papyrus roll, inkpot and pen. Hapuseneb gestured to him and he seated himself cross-legged at the priest's feet, and immediately set to work writing on the papyrus.

After a moment, he dusted the papyrus sheet with sand and offered it to Hapuseneb, who glanced at it and then held it up to the crowd. "The name of His Majesty, Hatshepsut, has been entered in the leaves of the sacred *isd-tree*. May his reign be long and fruitful!"

Excited whispers arose from the crowd. Hattie turned and accompanied Hapuseneb back into the temple, scores of glittering nobles and imposing officers descending from their chariots and following close on their heels. She caught a quick glimpse of Senemut in the crowd behind her. He grinned, and her heart leapt.

Hapuseneb led Hattie to a massive golden image of Amun, supported on a pallet by four burly, sweating priests. Hattie knelt before the image and lowered her head, as Senemut had instructed her, while Hapuseneb chanted a blessing. "Behold, Amun has come, and he has established the crown on the head of his worthy son, Hatshepsut, the protector of Egypt."

Hattie arose and led the image and the crowd into the innermost chamber of the temple—the most holy place, seen only by high priests, royalty and nobles. The room was dark and close with smoke from the flickering torches; sparks of light glinted and flashed from golden images of the gods. The scent of incense was heavy and cloying.

She knelt again. Hapuseneb lifted from the altar the unwieldy double crown of Upper and Lower Egypt and placed it on her head. The White Crown of Upper Egypt resembled a tall, bulbous bowling pin, and was surrounded by the chair-shaped Red Crown of Lower Egypt. Together, they represented her dominion over all of Egypt. A golden cobra with spread hood, representing pharaoh's protection by the gods, reared out from the crown over her brow. Hattie clenched her teeth and tightened her neck muscles to keep her head erect as she rose, bearing the weight of the tall, cold crown. If it fell from her head at her coronation, her reign would begin under a cloud of superstition from which it might never recover.

At last, she turned and faced the assembled group. A mighty shout of joy arose from nobles and priests alike. Hattie passed through their ranks, led the group out of the temple and paused, facing the buzzing crowd of peasants, servants and slaves.

Hapuseneb raised his hands and the people fell silent. "Behold— Amun has spoken. He has established the crown of Egypt on the head of His Majesty, Powerful of Kas, flourishing of years, divine of diadems, Maatkare, Khenmet-Amun Hatshepsut!"

As one, the crowd fell to its knees, hands outspread, foreheads in the dust.

Hattie Williams was now Hatshepsut, Pharaoh, and sole ruler of all Egypt.

CHAPTER 18

Hattie's head ached fiercely, and she thought she would die if she had to listen to another interminable toast praising her royal, sacred self. Smoke, perfume, incense, and food odors assaulted her in waves. Great Amun, she was pharaoh, yet she couldn't even send for an aspirin.

Shifting irritably on her chair, she looked around the low-ceilinged, torchlit room. Nobles and priests seated on cushions or leaning against elaborately carved pillars talked quietly, but not to her. The servants standing behind them respectfully averted their gaze when she glanced their way. Harps whispered, tambourine-like *sistrums* jangled, flutes wailed and castanets clacked, adding to the tumult in her brain. Bejeweled dancing girls circled and gyrated in a dizzying swirl of colors in the center of the room, while acrobats leapt over each other and twisted themselves into human knots. Dish after endless dish was placed on the low table in front of Hattie and Tuthmosis: roasted fish, duck and quail, stewed figs, cheese, bread, lentils, fresh berries, and honey cakes. Goblets of wine and beer flowed like the Nile.

At least she was not required to wear the burdensome double crown, praise Amun; only a golden circlet with a uraeus of a rearing cobra adorned her pounding forehead. Blast this century, and the lack of painkillers! She wondered for the hundredth time how long a royal coronation banquet was supposed to last, and when she could safely seek the oblivion of her bedchamber.

Tuthmosis had glared at her from his seat next to her on the dais for the first two hours of the banquet, anger vying with tears for expression. Hattie knew he was unhappy she'd been named pharaoh, seemingly having stolen his crown from him, but she dared not explain why. He was only a child, and shouldn't have to bear the heavy burden of fearing for his life. Hattie tried to make small talk with him instead, but he stubbornly refused to open his mouth except to insert food. Eventually, tired of his glumness, she suggested he retire for the evening. He rose, turned his back and hurried out of the room without so much as a "good night".

Massaging her aching temples, Hattie caught sight of Senemut, seated across the room. He sipped from a nearly untouched goblet of date wine and spoke quietly with Lord Ineni and Chancellor Neshi, their dark heads inclined politely to his. Sighing, she vowed that would be one of her first duties as pharaoh—from now on, Senemut would be at her side at every royal function. She was pharaoh, was she not, and her word law?

He looked up at her, and took in her fatigue and drooping shoulders at a glance. Surreptitiously, he gestured for her to rise. Not knowing what he had in mind, but trusting him implicitly, she stood.

At once, the entire company rose to its feet, and then bowed deeply to Hattie. "I…I shall retire now," she stammered. Why had she not thought of this before? Perhaps there was an advantage or two to being the ruler, after all.

Whispers of "Amun go with you", accompanied her to the door.

It's over, Hattie thought wearily as she dropped down onto her bed. But a persistent little voice in the back of her mind contended, *It's just beginning*. Shaking her head and then regretting it when the pounding intensified, she clapped her hands for her servant and allowed herself to relax under Nesi's capable ministrations.

Hattie was in bed at last and nearly asleep when she heard a tentative cough outside her bedchamber door. "Come in." She sighed. Was she never to be left alone?

Her mood immediately brightened as Senemut strode into the room. "I am sorry. I see I have awakened you, Hattie. It can wait until morning." He turned to leave.

She pushed herself upright on the bed. "Nay, come in. I was just thinking of the ceremony today, and wondering if it will be enough to safeguard Tuthmosis. Not that he is grateful for my protection," she added, grinning wryly. "He is more withdrawn than ever, if that is possible. I do not blame him…he feels I have usurped his rightful position."

"Aye, the young prince is grim." Senemut frowned. "I fear his boredom and somber mood will only become worse as he watches you wield pharaoh's power, day after day. I think it would be best…but nay, I will not say it again. It has been a long day, and you need to rest. We can discuss it tomorrow."

Hattie sighed. "Nay, I know what you were about to say, and I confess you are right. It is time to send Tuthmosis to train with the army. I can no longer endure his glumness. Mayhap serving time with the army will give him something enjoyable and useful to do with his time. It will teach him obedience and respect for authority, if nothing else."

Senemut's face brightened. "Aye, I am sure it will! And it will be invaluable for his future role as pharaoh. I suggest you send all his servants and retainers along with him as well. In addition to keeping the young prince safe, it will ensure that everyone around Your Majesty is loyal to you, and you alone. You will sleep much more soundly, I vow."

Hattie laughed, picturing the furor if a teenaged boy in her own time arrived at a military academy with maids and butlers in tow. But the seriousness of the situation sobered her instantly. "Your advice is sound, as always," she said. "Please notify General Snefru of my decision tomorrow." She patted the bed next to her. "Come, sit with me, Senemut."

He hesitated, then took a seat next to her. Though he did not touch her, he was close enough that she could feel the warmth radiating from him. She shivered. "I…I have something to tell you, Senemut. Something I should have told you far earlier, I fear." She reached for his hand.

"What is it? I know you wished to tell me something this morning, before the ceremonies. Speak now. It will calm you."

Hattie opened her mouth, but nothing came out. What if he didn't believe her story? What if he *did* believe it, and feared her because he thought she possessed magical powers that enabled her to travel through time? Did they burn witches here? Or, worst of all—what if he was furious at her for her dishonesty, her lack in trust of him? What if he turned his back on her? She would be alone, marooned in a friendless, alien place and time.

She shuddered. *Better to get it over with quickly*, she thought, fixing her glance on Senemut's strong, brown hand over hers. "I am not…I am not Hatshepsut. My name is Hattie Williams, and I was born more than three thousand years into your future. Somehow, I was thrust backward in time, and into the body of the real Hatshepsut. I know not how it happened. Nor do I know how to return to my own time. I am trapped here."

She paused and risked a look at him. His eyes wide, his mouth open, he stared at her as if she had suddenly sprouted an extra head.

Then his features relaxed. "*Hai!* You are a minx, playing a joke on me. I must confess, it is a good one, but you cannot fool me. You have possessed magical powers since childhood, but this is inconceivable, even for you."

Hattie shook her head and squeezed his hand. "I am not joking, Senemut. I swear I am not! Ask me anything and I will answer. I must prove to you that I am telling the truth. I cannot bear the burden alone any longer."

Senemut narrowed his eyes. "I will play along, though I know not why you wish to prolong the farce. Let me see—what do you look like, in this future time? Surely, you do not look precisely like Hatshepsut?"

Hattie snorted. "Nay, I do not! She is much more beautiful than I. Wait…" She snatched up a pen and piece of papyrus, and quickly sketched herself as she looked in her own time, complete with short, layered hairstyle and wispy bangs. She paused, then added a button-down collar around her neck. "This is what I look like."

Senemut studied the drawing for a moment in silence. "This is the image of a lovely woman, Hattie, who looks much like Hatshepsut." He traced the curve of Hattie's cheek on the picture. "The cheeks are a bit rounder, the eyes larger, but there is a marked similarity." He frowned. "The clothing is odd, however, and the wig quite unusual!"

She chuckled. "That is not a wig. It is my own hair, and in my time, it is considered to be quite a fashionable style."

"Aye, well, it is strange, I grant you. But ignoring the superficial changes of clothing and hair, it is Hatshepsut." He held up the drawing. "This is not sufficient proof. Tell me—when were you born, and where?"

"I was born on January twelfth, in Chicago, Illinois, in the year 1968. I know that month and year means nothing to you, but it is three thousand years in the future."

"January? Chicago? I know nothing of these words. What is the location of this Chicago where you say you were born?"

"It is in the United States of America." Seeing his puzzled look, she hastily added, "A large country, far to the north and west of Egypt. It has not been discovered yet."

Senemut smiled. "You come from a land not yet discovered, in a year that has not yet arrived. You have quite an imagination, little one! And what do you do in this mythical land?"

"I am an artist," Hattie explained. "I was at work on a series of drawings for a book…er, a papyrus about Hatshepsut. The real Hatshepsut," she amended hastily. "I was doing a detailed sketch of a necklace that was supposed to have belonged to her when something happened. Just as I finished copying the last hieroglyph, a wave of dizziness passed over me, and I fell. I must have lost consciousness. When I awoke, I was here." She spread her hands helplessly. "You know the rest of the story."

"A necklace?" Comprehension dawned across his face. "The necklace you asked me about—the one with the golden figure of Horus. You say that necklace brought you here?"

Hattie nodded miserably. "I think so. It is the only explanation I can come up with. The necklace, the hieroglyphs, or both. Mayhap the hieroglyphs were some kind of chant or spell, and when I finished copying them, the spell was triggered. But I did not know how to read hieroglyphics then, so I know not what they said. And, unfortunately, though I clutched it as I fell, the necklace did not travel here with me. I am marooned here. I know not how to return to my own time. I have been forced to play the part of Hatshepsut in order to survive."

"You were never talented in art until the funeral of your husband, the Great God. Yet now your skills rival any artisan's." He frowned, tapping the drawing he still held against his palm. "And in this…this ingenious tale of yours, what has happened to the real Hatshepsut?"

"I know not. You said you thought she had died at the funeral of her husband. Mayhap she did indeed die of grief. Her spirit may have left her body, which enabled my spirit to enter it. After I touched the necklace and swooned, I encountered a ghostly figure who claimed to be Hatshepsut, though I did not believe it at the time, and I have felt a…a presence more than once, heard a voice whisper to me when the room was empty, give me advice." She shrugged, staring down at the soft, slender hands so unlike her own capable ones. "I only know that this is not *my* body, and this is not my time."

"Hatshepsut was ever a timid woman," Senemut muttered, shaking his head again. "She would not dare to look me straight in the eye, much less seize the throne of Horus for herself. Yet, she knew well how to read and write, but I myself taught you these things. And her spells were always small and inclined toward love potions to help her favorite servants. Nothing as ambitious as travel through time. And yet, she did have powers beyond those of other women." A spasm of pain distorted his face. "What of us, if this preposterous tale is true? I have allowed myself to feel… to believe that you feel for me…" He groaned, crumpling the drawing in his fist. "Great Amun, my head spins as if from too much date wine."

"Oh, Senemut, if you believe nothing else I've told you, you must believe that I…" She gulped. "I…I had not planned to tell you in this fashion, but I love you, Senemut. With all my heart and soul."

"Aye, so you say, but who are you? By all the gods, I swear, I am tempted to believe you. You sound sincere. But can this tale be true? Are you really a stranger from another time?"

"It is true, I swear it by…" She broke off as a look of horror crossed his face and he rose from the bed so hastily that he stumbled. "Senemut, what is it? What is wrong?"

"By Amun and Isis and all the gods, what have I done?" He backed away from her outstretched hands, moaning and making the sign of the sacred eye of Horus. "What have I done? I have put an imposter on the throne of Egypt!" He turned and fled the room.

"Senemut, wait!" Hattie cried. "Please, come back!"

But it was too late; he was gone.

* * *

Senemut paced back and forth feverishly along the bank of the lotus pool in the garden adjoining his apartments. His mind was bleak, black; he felt like he'd been kicked in the stomach and had his heart torn out for good measure. He couldn't think, couldn't speak. All he could do was walk and turn, walk and turn.

After a time, the mechanical activity soothed him a little. He dropped down onto a stone bench, his head in his hands. Great Amun, what had he done? He had allowed himself to be led about by his heart like a young, untried boy. He had fallen for a pretty face, a tender smile…or, he thought bitterly as he eyed the drawing Hattie had made, *I fell for two pretty faces.*

He shook his head viciously. Nay, he couldn't believe, even now, that he had acted only out of lust, or even love. Hatshepsut…nay, *Hattie*…was fit in every way to rule Egypt, except for her gender. And why should that keep an otherwise fit leader from the throne? Thus, he had been right to help her be crowned pharaoh.

Yet, the throne of Egypt was not a prize to be won by intelligence or leadership or even feat of arms. It was a sacred position that passed from father to son, along the royal line—and Hattie was not a member of the royal family. If her outlandish tale were true, that is. In that case, putting her on the throne was worse than an affront against Egypt; it was an affront against the gods, against *maat* itself: truth, justice, order, stability. Without *maat*, the universe would slide into chaos and disorder and the world would be destroyed.

Senemut stood and resumed pacing. Should he try to wrest the scepter from Hattie's grasp and give it into the hand of another? Perhaps that would restore *maat*. Yet, to try to unseat pharaoh was the worst sacrilege of all. Would that not destroy *maat* in and of itself?

"Amun help me," Senemut groaned aloud. "What am I to do?"

CHAPTER 19

Day after lonely day passed. Senemut did not reappear, and Hattie missed him sorely. When he hadn't returned after two days, she sent a servant, bearing an apologetic note, to inquire after him. The servant returned quickly, saying only that Lord Senemut was indisposed and would see no one. Her letter, pleading with him to listen to her, to give her a chance to explain, was returned unread.

Hattie knew that, as pharaoh, she could command his presence, yet she knew it would solve nothing. Indeed, it would be a grave mistake. He must come to an understanding of who she was, an acceptance of her, on his own, and she couldn't force it. So, she must wait, though it killed her to do so.

While she waited, there were many royal duties to keep her occupied. She presided at court, made the required appearances at the temple, spoke with the nobles. Without Senemut's counsel and sage advice, she didn't know if she performed the duties properly, nor did she care. She missed the sound of his voice, the brilliance of his smile, the warmth of his touch. Despite her best intentions, Hattie had admitted to Senemut and herself that she had fallen in love with him. And without his presence, her life in this alien land was nothing more than a burden.

The only bright spot in her life was little Neferure. The princess radiated delight, enthusiasm, and simple joy in life, and always brought a smile to Hattie's lips. As she held the child on her lap or sang her to sleep at night, she vowed she would never tell the truth to Neferure. Though it would be a weight on her soul until the day she died to impersonate the child's mother, she would not take away one ounce of the little girl's happiness and security, just to ease her own conscience.

Tuthmosis had been shipped off with General Snefru to train with the army, far to the south, where he would remain for several years. Any guilt Hattie might have felt at sending the boy away was instantly erased when Tuthmosis came to her before he left and gave an awkward speech of thanks, carefully prepared and memorized. He even smiled at her briefly, the first genuine smile he'd bestowed since her arrival. As always, Senemut was right. Sending Tuthmosis away had been the proper thing to do. What would she do now, without Senemut's counsel and advice?

Hattie was seated in her bedchamber, disconsolately practicing her hieroglyphs, when the curtain flapped aside and Senemut strode in. "Majesty," he said, nodding briefly.

"Senemut!" She flew to his side and reached out for him, tears of joy welling in her eyes. She could scarcely breathe and her heart felt like it would burst.

He held up a hand to stop her advance. "I have things to tell you, things I must say. Pray, do me the courtesy of listening to them without interruption."

The hope within her quickly withered at his gruff tone. "Of course," she whispered, sinking down onto the stool.

"I have thought long and hard on all you have told me," he said, pacing back and forth across the small open space in the room. "I did not wish to accept it. I tried to find another explanation for your story, any explanation at all. But alas, I fear you spoke the truth. I believe you are not Hatshepsut, but instead a woman from another time and place. I know not how you came here or why, but it is plain that you are who you claim to be."

Hattie sagged with relief. At least he accepted her story, for good or ill. She felt like a tremendous burden had been removed from her shoulders.

"Since you are not the real Hatshepsut, I have made a grievous error in having you crowned. I have placed a stranger, a woman—and one not of royal blood!—on the throne of Egypt. I know not if the gods will forgive me for this…this abomination."

She opened her mouth to speak, but he held up his hand again.

"What is done cannot be easily undone, I fear. I cannot take the crown from your head, any more than I can raise the dead. The only way to remove you from the throne of Horus is through your death."

Hattie shifted uneasily on her stool. This one-sided conversation was not going as well as she had hoped. Was Senemut still angry with her? Angry enough to have her killed, or to kill her himself? Had she been mistaken about his ability to absorb and accept her revelation?

"Amun preserve me, but I cannot wish for your death." When he met her gaze at last, an electric shock coursed through her. "You are a helpless toy of the gods, as am I. I know not what they have in mind, but I must trust there is a plan, else they would not have brought you here."

"I hope so," she murmured, dropping her gaze. Her cheeks were flushed and her heart raced. Now the conversation was venturing into safer territory.

"Aye, mayhap it is best thus," Senemut said, resuming his pacing. "The gods have not struck me down yet and mayhap they will not. Tuthmosis is too young to rule. Were you not on the throne, a Regent would be appointed and I cannot imagine one of his advisors in that position. Between them, they have the wisdom of a single, obstinate donkey."

Hattie giggled at the image his words presented. After a moment, Senemut's rich laugh joined hers. The tension in the air dissipated, and she relaxed a little. Perhaps everything would be all right after all.

Senemut crossed the floor to her in two steps, seized her by the arms, and hauled her upright. Her heart thudded in her chest as he held her so close to him that she was enfolded by his spicy, masculine scent as the warmth of his body radiated and enveloped her.

"By the gods, I have missed your laugh," he said, staring down into her face with a strange expression she couldn't quite decipher. "I have realized something else these days past. If you are not Hatshepsut, then I can touch you. I can hold you. I can love you."

She held her breath for a moment before she let it out on a soft sigh. "Aye," she whispered. "And I can love you, too, Senemut. I *do* love you."

A small eternity passed, a moment frozen in time, as she stared up at him. Then Senemut pulled her even closer, one arm around her waist, the other hand cupping the back of her head. "My love," he breathed, then slanted his lips down over hers.

Fire leapt through Hattie's veins as she returned his kiss, feeling a passion she hadn't known she possessed. She wrapped her arms around his neck, her knees suddenly weak and trembling. He lifted her easily and carried her to the bed. As his body covered hers, a surge of delight shot through her, which was instantly replaced by a deeper, more intense feeling than she had ever experienced. It was a sense of rightness, of...of *maat*. All was well with the world, and she was where she belonged: in Senemut's arms.

CHAPTER 20

"Hattie?"

"Hmm?" Hattie raised her head sleepily from Senemut's chest and opened one eye.

"We must talk."

She closed her eye. "Later, after we sleep." She nestled close again and pressed a kiss onto his collarbone.

"You should marry again."

Hattie sat bolt upright. "Senemut! Is that a marriage proposal? If it is, the answer is aye. Aye!"

Senemut sighed and toyed with one of her red-gold braids. "Nay. I fear I cannot marry you, as much as I would wish it. We must find another—mayhap a foreign prince—for you to marry. Someone who will not lust after the throne himself."

Hattie's jaw dropped and she glared at him. "That is preposterous! Surely you know I will never marry another? You are the only one in my heart."

"As you are in mine," he said, caressing her cheek. "But I am not of noble birth, and thus I am not suitable to be your husband. We cannot reveal to anyone that you are not the real Hatshepsut, so your husband's background must be beyond question."

"What do you mean, you are not suitable? You are entirely suitable! I think I am capable of making that decision… especially after last night." She grinned.

Senemut's face remained stubbornly serious. "I am not of noble birth. A marriage between us would never be accepted by the priests, the nobles, or the people. We have stretched their credibility to put you on the throne. They will not accept a commoner married to a female pharaoh."

"Blast the people!" she cried, throwing her hands up in the air. "I care not what they will accept. I refuse to marry another. It would be a sacrilege to do so, for your love is sacred to me. You are the only one I will ever love."

"And you are my only love," he repeated patiently. "But think, Hattie—what if there is a child?"

Hattie gasped. The issue of birth control had totally escaped her last night, and even had it not, there were no conveniently-situated pharmacies in this time and place. For all she knew, she was carrying Senemut's child at this moment. "I had not thought of that," she confessed. "But, Senemut, I would be delighted to bear your children, whether we can marry or not." She firmly pushed away the thought of giving birth in this medically primitive, germ-ridden era. She would cross that bridge when she came to it.

"Nay, my love, you cannot bear my children unless you are married. That is why we must find you a husband."

"How can you expect me to marry a man I do not love? It would not be fair to him. It would not be fair to me! And to expect him to claim your children as his own, and raise them… Senemut, that is too much to ask. Nay, I will not do it. If I cannot marry you, then I will not marry at all."

Senemut sighed. "Then we must be sure there *are* no children. I will have my private physician prepare the necessary items, and you must use them every time we…each time we are together."

"Of course I will," she agreed, silently amending, *If they aren't too unpleasant.* She had seen physicians use remedies that contained bull's urine, crocodile dung, and other nasty ingredients, and she had no intention of coming within shouting distance of one of those.

"And," he continued relentlessly, "we must make sure there is no child now."

"What do you mean?" Suspicion suddenly coiled around her heart like a vise.

"I will have my physician make up an elixir that will cause you to lose the baby, should there be one." He winced as he spoke the words, and a spasm of grief passed over his face.

"Nay, Senemut!" she cried. "If I carry your child now, I will not lose it. I will not!" She burst into tears. How could he ask such a thing of her? Her heart throbbed painfully and felt like it would break. She had never craved a child, but suddenly she wanted a child of Senemut's, yearned for it with every fiber of her being.

He gathered her in his arms. "It is hard, I know, little one," he said, stroking her back and her hair. "The will of the gods is hard. But I fear it must be so."

"Nay, I will not," she sobbed. "I will not. If I bear your child, then I will raise it—and the gods be damned!"

"Hush, now. You must not affront the gods, for their vengeance is swift. We shall wait a little, shall we? Mayhap it will not be necessary after all. Let us wait and see if there is a child."

She sniffled and nodded against his chest. "Aye. We will wait." *But if I carry your child, I will find a way to keep it*, she vowed silently. *I will not throw away the best thing that has happened to me, gods or no gods.*

Fortunately for Hattie, there was no child. But she felt little relief, for there was an empty place in her heart that would have been filled by Senemut's babies, and now would always be barren and lonely. Why had she traveled to this accursed century? Surely, not just to have her heart broken. Hatshepsut's directives to her about protecting Tuthmosis and uncovering the traitors seemed distant and unimportant compared to her overwhelming grief.

Senemut tried to cheer her, but there was little he could do. The only ray of sunshine in her life was little Neferure. Now that Hattie dared not bear children of her own, she expended all the maternal love she had on the child, who returned it tenfold. In time, Neferure's unreserved cheerfulness and devotion healed the wound, and Hattie's naturally buoyant spirit returned. She would always carry a scar, but at least she had one child to lavish her attention upon.

Senemut came to her one night a few weeks later, bearing the contraceptive devices his physician had fashioned, carefully secreted in a small alabaster box.

"What are they made of?" She eyed the damp, gray wads of

unidentifiable material suspiciously.

"They are wool, moistened with honey, and mixed with ground acacia and dates," he explained. "Nothing more."

"Nothing more? Are you certain?" She lifted one out of the box and sniffed it cautiously. There was no telltale odor of dung or other disagreeable ingredients. "And what am I to do with this... this sticky thing? Swallow it?"

Senemut burst into laughter. "Nay, right before we...you must take it and place it in your...*hai*, never mind. I will show you." He caught her up in his arms and carried her to the bed.

Hattie giggled. "Please do."

"It is good to hear you laugh again!" Senemut exclaimed. "You have been so distraught these past few weeks, and it has pierced my heart like a dagger. I am glad to see joy returning to your face." He smiled down at her, his face full of tenderness and love.

She reached up and stroked his cheek. "I cannot be unhappy for long when I am in your presence."

"Oh, is that true? Well, then, let me demonstrate for you how this device works." He grinned.

"Aye, Senemut. Show me," she murmured.

* * *

The next morning, Hattie felt well rested and more cheerful than she had in weeks. "What shall we do today?" she asked Senemut, as she slipped into her gown.

"Today, we must plan the first accomplishment of your reign," he answered. "A military campaign, I think. Mayhap against Canaan? They have not felt the wrath of Egypt's sword for many a season."

"A campaign? Nay. Definitely not." She shuddered. "I will not send men to their death again."

"But Pharaoh Maatkare Khenmet-Amun Hatshepsut must prove his strength," he protested. "Else the vassal states will take it as a sign of weakness, and rebel."

"There are other ways to prove that Egypt is mighty, and a force to be reckoned with. It is not necessary to use brute force," Hattie insisted. "If I am to remain pharaoh, then my reign will be a peaceful one, if possible. We will deal with other nations on an equal basis. We will trade with them, invite them to send ambassadors to our court, and we will protect them, if necessary. We will make them all our allies and our friends."

"*Ast!*" Senemut struck the heel of his hand to his forehead. "That policy will bring Egypt down in ruins, crumbling around our ears! You must be strong, Hattie. There must be a campaign."

She shook her head. "Nay. There will be no campaign. At least, not now," she temporized, seeing the genuine despair on his face. "Let us give my plan a try. If it does not work—if, in a year or two, rebellions crop up—I will follow your advice and launch a campaign. But we will try my way first. Please, Senemut?"

He paced back and forth like a caged lion, glancing at her occasionally and then turning away and shaking his head. At last, he stopped directly in front of her. "I agree. We will try your reign of peace for one year. But—" He held up a finger in warning, his face stern. "—if during that time a rebellion occurs, you must order out your army to quell it. I do not wish to see my country defeated and laughed at."

"Egypt is my country now, too," she protested softly. "I would not see her defeated. Very well, Senemut, I agree to your terms." She held out her hand.

Senemut stared at her extended hand skeptically. "What is that for?"

Hattie couldn't suppress a grin. "Where I come from, when people who trust one another come to an agreement, they shake hands to seal the bargain. Will you shake hands with me on our arrangement?"

He shook his head. "A silly custom, but I will indulge you." He took her hand in his, and they shook. Then he grasped her arm with his other hand and pulled her close. "In *my* country, we have a much more pleasant way of sealing a bargain between a man and a woman," he murmured.

She raised her face to his. "I would like to learn this custom," she breathed. "Teach me."

"Aye, Your Majesty. It will be my pleasure." He leaned down, but stopped with his lips a tantalizing inch from hers. "But then we must decide what your first royal accomplishment shall be."

"That is easy," Hattie said, remembering a small portion of ancient Egyptian history. "We shall send a trading expedition to Punt."

"Punt? Your first accomplishment will be an expedition to a mythical land? By the sacred beard of Ptah, I think I was foolish to agree to your scheme." He scowled down at her.

"Trust me," she insisted. "Punt does exist, and my expedition there will be a great success. It will be spoken of for many generations."

His eyes narrowed. "Oh, aye? Well, mayhap it will at that. I must remember that you have traveled here from the future, and know what is to happen. And do you know what I intend to do to you now?"

She smiled warmly. "I do not need to see into the future to determine that."

* * *

Hattie tapped her foot impatiently, waiting for the ceremony to begin. The Atef ceremonial crown, similar to the White Crown of Upper Egypt in shape and color but decorated with white ostrich feathers, pressed heavily on her forehead, and she felt the beginnings of a headache creep into her temples. The midday air was stifling under the summer sun, without even a hint of a cooling breeze. She wished she were still inside the temple, where at least the stone and mud-brick walls kept it a little cooler.

Earlier, before the heat had grown unbearable, she had participated in the ceremony to bless her expedition to Punt. Hapuseneb conducted the ceremony at the temple complex at Karnak, in the beautiful Red Chapel which Senemut had constructed in Hatshepsut's name. The small red-quartzite chapel was the sanctuary of the sacred barque of Amun, *Userhat-Amun*, "Mighty of Prow is Amun". The barque was a small, gilded wooden barge on which the statue of Amun was transported by priests from the temple at Karnak to the temple at Luxor and back again on feast days and special occasions. Under Hapuseneb's direction, both Hattie and Chancellor Neshi, the leader of the

Punt expedition, offered incense to Amun and prayed for his blessing on the voyage. Then Neshi hurried away, as quickly as he could without offending the gods, to oversee the final preparations for the first leg of the expedition.

Now Hattie stood atop the immense pylon at the entrance to Karnak with Hapuseneb on her right and Senemut behind. The pylon, decorated with colorful murals and topped with pennants hanging limp in the still, sweltering air, gave her a perfect vantage point to watch Chancellor Neshi scurrying to and fro as five small, unassembled ships were loaded onto ox-drawn carts just east of the temple complex. Other carts were laden with trade goods: bolts of fine Egyptian linen, polished bronze and copper mirrors, dozens of beaded necklaces and bracelets, small axes and daggers, and cask after cask of Egyptian wine and beer. One cart carried water and food for the travelers' consumption on the trip.

Scores of sweating soldiers and oarsmen swarmed around the carts, getting underfoot more often than not, to judge by Neshi's bellowing. His commanding voice rose clearly to Hattie above the clamor. Senemut had obviously been wise to suggest that Neshi lead the expedition.

At last, the hubbub died down a little, and Neshi turned to look up at Hattie. He raised his staff and bowed.

Hattie rose. "Go forth to the land of Punt," she said, her arms outstretched to the caravan below, though she knew they couldn't hear her words. "Amun will lead you, by land and by water, to the mysterious shores of the fabled land. Trade with the inhabitants you find there, for the glory of Hatshepsut and of all Egypt. Return with incense trees for my father Amun's temple, and all manner of goods. May Amun guide and protect you on your perilous voyage!" She held aloft the sacred crook and flail, crossed, in blessing.

Neshi bowed again, then turned and shouted a command to the cart drivers. They flicked their whips and the carts lurched forward as the oxen plodded away from Thebes and into the desert. They had a long, grueling journey of a hundred miles or more through the eastern desert before they reached the Red Sea, where they would assemble the boats and travel south to find Punt.

Hattie sank down gratefully into a small stool. "At last they are underway," she murmured. "Now we can get out of the heat."

"You are certain they will return?" Senemut asked her for the hundredth time since she had proposed the excursion. "The journey is long and dangerous, even before they reach the sea. And the sea itself is a treacherous place to send any man. More dangerous by far than the battlefield."

"But you travel in ships on the Nile, and do not think it dangerous," she protested. "Why are Egyptians so afraid of the Red Sea?"

"The Nile is our mother. It provides us with food for our table and clothing for our bodies. But the sea—this Red Sea, as you call it—is vast and uncharted, and full of unknown dangers." Senemut shook his head. "You call it Red. Mayhap it is red with the blood of all the men it has swallowed up?"

She tried to stifle a grin. "Nay, I am sure it is due to a mineral deposit, something that is red in color. Nothing more sinister than that. Aye, they will return safely, though the voyage will take nearly a year. I promise, Senemut."

Senemut looked unconvinced. "I will hold you to that promise, Hattie," he said.

CHAPTER 21

"*A*i, she will ruin us!" Snefru moaned bitterly, his head in his hands. "I come home from months of training to find she has chosen her first official act. And what is that act? A campaign... against Syria, mayhap, which grows overbold? A new taxation to fill Egypt's coffers? Even a new temple for herself?" He shook his head. "Nay. She chooses a trading expedition—to Punt! A land that only exists in tales to frighten small children. By all the gods, she will make Egypt a laughing stock."

"Have patience, friend," Hapuseneb said, gripping Snefru's arm and shaking it. "She but ties the rope more securely around her own neck. The nobles are aghast at this wanton waste of men and resources and, as you know, the army grows restless for lack of action. They have not seen battle since the campaign in Nubia. When her little expedition returns empty-handed—or when they fail to return at all—the peasants will turn on her as well. It has been many months since the expedition departed, and there has been no hint of its return."

"But the peasants love her," Snefru put in. "There is no explanation for it, but the fact exists. She has the strong support of the commoners, and that is a point we must not overlook. They throng the streets whenever she appears. They throw lotus blossoms at her feet. And they love Senemut, who is one of their own, yet has risen to greatness."

"Aye, they love her because she is *kind* to them." Hapuseneb pronounced "kind" as if it were a curse. To be kind was the last quality a pharaoh should exhibit. "She provides bread for their hungry bellies, clothes for their scantily-clad bodies. But they do not *respect* her. To earn respect, pharaoh must be firm and commanding, strong and ruthless. Not weak and soft. When her expedition fails, they will see this. I expect news any day that the expedition has been destroyed in wild foreign lands."

"Mayhap," Snefru muttered. "But it may not be so easy to sway the minds of the peasants. They are a stolid and singularly unimaginative lot, and as you said, she feeds and clothes them."

"Just to be safe, we will not wait for news that her foolish expedition to Punt has failed. Tonight, we will put our primary plan into action."

Snefru rose from his stool, a wide grin spreading across his face. "You mean…?"

Hapuseneb chuckled. Trust Snefru to be enthusiastic about any type of action, regardless of the end result. "Aye. Tonight, her favorite, the common-born Senemut, dies."

* * *

Hattie heard a polite cough outside her chambers. "Come in," she said.

An unfamiliar servant entered and bowed low. The palace was overrun with servants. There was no way to recognize each and every one.

"What is it? You may rise."

"Majesty, the Lord Senemut, Steward of Amun, bids you join him in Your Highness's private lotus garden for an evening walk," the servant said, keeping his face averted from hers. He spoke as if he had carefully rehearsed his lines.

"He does?" Hattie frowned. "Why did he not say as much to me? Why does he send a messenger?"

"I know not, Divine One," the servant murmured. "I have only done as I was instructed…nothing more."

"Of course, of course," Hattie said. Most of the servants were afraid to speak in her presence; at least this one answered her questions. "Thank you. You may go."

The servant bowed deeply, turned and left the room.

"Why did he not come here and ask me himself?" Hattie said aloud. Shrugging, she slipped on her sandals and snatched a white woolen cloak from a carved cedar chest. Egyptian night air was sometimes chilly. Wrapping the cloak around her, she hastened to the entrance of the private walled garden.

The air in the garden was delightfully cool, and carried the scent of lotus blossoms that crowded the small, rectangular pool. Ducks and geese quacked and flapped their wings as they settled down for the night on the grassy banks of the pool. Acacia, date palm and fig trees nodded around the borders of the tiny garden, adding deep shadows to the already-murky environment.

In the dim light of the crescent moon, Hattie thought she could make out a figure seated on a stone bench under a fig tree. "Senemut? Is that you?" she called.

The figure rose and came toward her. "Aye, Hattie." He put his arms around her and embraced her. "Did you miss me?"

"Of course," she murmured against his shoulder. "I always miss you when you are not with me." She lifted her face to his and smiled. "What a lovely idea, to walk in the garden at night, away from prying eyes. I am so happy you thought of it!"

"I thought of it? *Hai*, you and your jokes," Senemut muttered as he claimed her lips with his.

Hattie pushed on his chest and leaned back in his arms. "What do you mean, jokes? Did you not send me a message asking me to meet you here?"

Senemut frowned. "Nay, I sent you no such message."

"Then why are you here?"

"Because I received a message from *you*, asking that I meet you here. I believe the message said you wanted to discuss an important matter of state. Did you not send this message?"

"Nay, I did not." A duck quacked nearby and Hattie's heart jumped to her throat. "What is happening? Someone is manipulating us, and I fear it is for an evil purpose."

"I am afraid you may be right. Who brought you this message that you were told was from me?"

"A servant. I did not recognize him and he kept his face averted from me." She grimaced. "I should have been suspicious of his behavior. Most servants fear me, yet he appeared unafraid to answer my questions."

"It is not your fault," Senemut murmured. "Why should you be suspicious? You say he was a servant. What did he look like?"

"I did not see his face," she repeated. "He wore a common, coarsely-woven kilt. He had no wig, and his head was shaved. He was of medium height and build." She spread her hands helplessly. "I fear I can tell you nothing more. I paid him scant attention."

"Hmm. That sounds like the messenger who brought me the request to join you here. Tell me, did he give you a written message, or was it spoken?"

"The message was spoken," Hattie said, then sighed. "It seemed strange you would contact me thus, but I thought mayhap you were busy."

"And I thought the same," Senemut confessed. Suddenly, he whirled around. "*Ast!* Did you hear that?"

"Aye," she whispered, her heart lurching again. "I think it came from over there in the corner under the acacia tree…"

At that moment, a dark figure burst out from under the tree she had pointed to, heading straight for Senemut and Hattie.

"Run, Hattie!" Senemut yelled over his shoulder as he turned to meet the threat.

Hattie, however, had no intention of abandoning him. She stood frozen, not sure what was happening or how to react. Then she saw something that turned her blood to ice. The intruder racing toward Senemut had raised his hand and the pale moonlight glinted on the blade of a wicked-looking knife clenched in his fist. "Watch out! He has a knife!" she shouted.

Senemut grasped the intruder's arms and they struggled fiercely, silently. Hattie moved around the two, trying to get behind the assailant so she could trip him.

"Run!" Senemut repeated, turning his gaze to her for an instant.

That instant was all the attacker needed. Jerking free the hand that gripped the knife, he plunged it down into Senemut's chest, then turned and, climbing the acacia tree with the agility of a monkey, jumped over the wall and vanished.

Senemut groaned and slumped to the ground.

"Senemut!" Hattie rushed to him and lifted his head onto her lap. "Are you all right? Speak to me, please!" She felt warm blood flowing from the wound in his chest. Tearing off her cloak, she wadded it up and pressed it against the wound, holding it in place with both hands.

His eyelids fluttered open. "I…I am sorry, Hattie…" he whispered. "Sorry I could not…could not protect you." He raised his hand to her face, then he closed his eyes and his hand dropped onto her lap.

"Nay, Senemut," she cried, tears flowing down her cheeks. "You cannot leave me! I need you. You must not die!"

Senemut didn't respond. He was unconscious…or dead?

"Guards!" she screamed. "Guards! Come to me at once!"

Almost immediately, the sound of clattering footsteps converged on her position. Cradling Senemut's head on her lap, she allowed her tears to rain down and mix with his blood, which oozed slowly through her cloak and between her outspread fingers. She prayed, as she had never prayed before, that Senemut could be saved. If he couldn't, she would be left to rule Egypt friendless and alone, without the man she trusted—and without the man she loved.

* * *

"It is done, my friend." Hapuseneb smiled broadly at the surprise evident on Snefru's face, quickly replaced by triumph. "Senemut is finished. The assassin has already been sent to meet the gods, so none will be the wiser to our involvement."

Snefru rubbed his hands together with glee. "Amun be praised! And she will be next, will she not?"

"Aye. But you must have patience," Hapuseneb cautioned. "We must not draw any undue attention to ourselves. Return to your post with the army and say nothing. Do not indicate you have any knowledge of Senemut's death. We must wait for the news to spread in a natural fashion." He needed to keep Snefru calm. Amun forbid, Snefru should blunder and give them away now.

"I know how to handle myself," Snefru grumbled, glaring at him. "You have little faith in me, priest."

"And with good reason," Hapuseneb retorted. Great Amun,

who did this…this *soldier* think he was, treating him with such disrespect? "What we do is punishable by death—the most hideous, painful kind of death. I, for one, do not wish to die in such a fashion."

"Nor do I wish this," Snefru said, holding up his hands. "Fear not, I shall remain as silent as the dead. But I wish to know when you will make your move against Hatshepsut. My patience grows weary."

"Do not worry," Hapuseneb said, smiling thinly. Once again, he had brought Snefru into line, but the sooner this was over, the better. He had no intention of letting this blundering fool ruin him. "Without Senemut whispering in her ear, our little pharaoh will soon allow the governing of Egypt to flounder. She is not fit for such work.

"And once the people see her for what she is—a weak, silly woman—they will do our work for us. Hatshepsut will be no more, our hands will be clean, and the rightful heir will take the throne of the Two Lands, with his trusted advisors by his side."

CHAPTER 22

Senemut was not dead, but he might as well have been, for all the royal physician could do for him. The physician placed sacred scarabs carved from alabaster and other charms on various parts of his body, chanted prayers to numerous gods, and fastened a protective bracelet around each wrist. When, at last, he attempted to place a noxious-smelling salve on the wound, Hattie could stand no more. She ordered him out of the room and he left, though he cast more than one perplexed glance behind him.

"Blast this primitive culture," she muttered when he had gone. "Senemut, I am sorry, but you will have to make do with me as your physician. My own physician is no better than a witch doctor. I vow on my life I will save you, my dearest love. I will not lose you now!"

Senemut groaned, but didn't open his eyes. He lay in her bed, where she had bade the guards carry him, floating in and out of consciousness. At least the bleeding had stopped.

Gently, Hattie stripped the torn and bloodstained cloak and kilt from his body. Then, using a bowl of water and a clean linen rag, she bathed the wound as best she could. It was high up on the left side of his chest. It was a miracle it had missed his heart and, apparently, his lungs as well. It seemed to be a clean thrust, and she prayed that meant there would be no infection.

"Senemut, I must disinfect your wound," she murmured, not knowing if he could hear her. "I fear it will hurt, and for that, I am sorry. But it must be done." Wincing, she poured a small amount of wine directly over the wound, then blotted the area and poured a bit more. Senemut made no sound…he was unconscious again.

Sighing, Hattie took clean strips of linen and bound the injury as best she could. What she wouldn't give for some penicillin!

Senemut was deathly pale, and he had lost a great deal of blood. Since there was no possibility of a blood transfusion, Hattie knew all she could do was try to keep the wound clean and free from infection, and get some nourishment into him so his body could concentrate all its energies on healing. But what food would be best? What food could he tolerate? Certainly, he couldn't sit up and chew.

She called for her head chef. He came to her almost at once. "I want you to prepare something special and nourishing for Lord Senemut," she said.

"Of course, Your Majesty. What shall I make?" he asked, bowing.

"Take a good piece of beef. Take care that it has little fat on it. Put it in a pot and cover it with water; then, cover the pot and cook it over the fire until the meat falls from the bones."

The chef nodded. "And shall I bring you this boiled meat?"

Hattie shook her head. "Nay. Use the special sieve my baker uses to sift the flour, and strain the meat and bones from the broth. Take care you save the broth in a clean container, and bring it to me. You may discard the meat and bones, or use the meat as you choose in another dish."

"Just the liquid, Your Majesty?" The chef seemed puzzled. "Surely, there is more nourishment in the meat itself, or in the bone marrow?"

"Aye, you may be correct," she said. "But Lord Senemut will only be able to tolerate liquids for some time yet, I fear."

"As you wish, Radiant One. I shall see to it immediately." The chef bowed again and departed.

For the next three days, Hattie didn't leave Senemut's side. She bathed and dressed his wound several times a day, and fed him spoonfuls of broth whenever he appeared conscious. She slept in a chair next to the low bed, one arm draped across him so she would awaken immediately if he moved or needed something. Nesi stayed on guard outside the door, turning away visitors and responding promptly to Hattie's every request.

On the evening of the third day, Senemut appeared to be resting easier and his color was much improved. Hattie dropped off into a deep slumber, her first real sleep since he had been stabbed.

Hattie awoke to the sound of birds singing. She opened her eyes a slit. Sunlight streamed in through the high window of her room. Gasping, she leapt to a stand. How could she have slept the night through without checking once on Senemut?

She looked down on him, fearful of what she might find. His eyes were open and he watched her with a faint smile. "Must you make so much noise in the room of a sick man?" he whispered. "Your leaping about makes my head pound." He winked.

"Senemut!" She dropped to her knees next to the bed and took his hand, pressing it to her cheek. "Thank Amun, you are awake! How do you feel?"

"I feel as if a hippopotamus has been using me for a chair," he grumbled. Then his expression softened. "I have had strange dreams and visions, but in all of them you were there, safeguarding me. I thank you for my life. I know I owe it to you and your vigilance."

Hattie stroked his forehead. "You will be all right now. Your wound is healing. You are fortunate it pierced no vital organs. All you need is nourishing food and rest."

"I have rested enough," he said. "But food...I confess, I am hungry enough to eat a crocodile."

"I can remedy that." Hattie clapped her hands and Nesi appeared at once.

"Aye, Majesty?"

"Bring some of the special bread, roasted fish, and wine for Lord Senemut," she told the servant.

Nesi scurried away and soon returned with the tray of food. Hattie helped Senemut maneuver to a semi-upright position, then fed him morsels of food and sips of wine. At last, he raised his hand. "I cannot hold more," he said with a sigh. "That was the best meal I can recall."

"I am so happy to see you awake and eating," Hattie said. "You will grow stronger now, and soon you will be back on your feet. Senemut, I was afraid I would lose you." She clasped his hand and pressed it to her heart. "I could not survive without you! Promise me you will be more careful in the future."

"Aye, Your Majesty. I promise," he said, smiling. "I must see to your safety as you saw to mine. I cannot afford to be weak and ill. I must guard you."

"We shall guard each other," Hattie declared.

CHAPTER 23

"This is preposterous!" Hapuseneb roared. "How is it that Senemut still lives?" He paced across the floor, then turned to face Snefru. "Are the gods against us? Are we doomed to fail with each attempt we make?"

"I know not," Snefru said irritably. "It seems there is a greater power watching over those two, else they would both be dead by now. But I remain confident we can find a way to rid ourselves of them, if we do not concede defeat."

"I am not so sure." Hapuseneb slumped onto a chair. Every attempt he'd made had been thwarted, every effort neatly sidestepped. Was he angering the gods in his attempt to dethrone Hatshepsut? "I think mayhap we are attempting the impossible. The gods must wish that woman to stay on the throne. If they do not wish so, why have we not succeeded? Senemut was stabbed and should have died, yet he is recovering and regaining his strength."

Senemut was recovering his strength, no doubt, due to an unfortunate combination of his strong constitution, lack of skill on the part of the assassin, and Hatshepsut refusing the services of the physician Hapuseneb had bribed. But he had no intention of making Snefru aware of his other operatives. The man was much too rash to be trusted with such information "Or mayhap it is not the gods," he added. "Possibly Hatshepsut herself has some magic powers we are unaware of, beyond her simple love spells and charms."

"Aye, that might be it." Snefru nodded thoughtfully. "Perchance we err in trying to rid ourselves of her through mortal means. We might be better served through using magic. But—" He thumped

130

his chest. "—I am no sorcerer. I am a soldier, and the only means I have at my disposal are men and weapons. If there is to be magic, you must provide it, Hapuseneb."

Hapuseneb's eyes brightened and he straightened. At last, the fool had come up with a valuable suggestion! "I think you are right. We must dispose of her with a spell of some kind. I dare not try to put a poison into her drink this time. She would suspect as much. Possibly a spell on an object of some kind?" He nodded thoughtfully and pursed his lips. "Aye, that might do it."

"I will leave that to you. In the meantime, I will wait for an opportunity to strike again at Senemut. No matter how powerful her magic is, she cannot be watchful all the time. Sooner or later, I will find an opportunity, and I will seize it." Snefru smiled like a crocodile about to devour a tender gazelle that had wandered too close to the water. "I am confident we will succeed yet."

* * *

"You treat me like an infant," Senemut grumbled. "I am tired of being confined to this room. I wish to walk through the palace, or mayhap sit in the garden. I need fresh air!"

Hattie shuddered. "I do not think I can endure that garden, and I wish you would avoid it also. I confess I am reluctant to leave this room, since we know not who your would-be assassin was, or who sent him."

He stroked her cheek. "I understand, little warrior. You have been so brave! But we cannot live our lives in fear. We must be cautious, but we must go on."

"I suppose you are right." She sighed. "Very well, let us take a stroll through the palace. We will prove you are alive and well, and that the traitors did not succeed in taking your life. Mayhap they will think twice before trying again. But I have no intention of visiting the garden."

"That is a fair bargain." Senemut rose slowly and crossed the room to her. "You see? I am strong. You need not worry."

Hattie winced as she watched him move painfully to her side, but she kept her voice light. "Aye, I see. Soon you will be hauling enormous limestone blocks to my mortuary temple on your back!

I have no doubt." She smiled. "Come, we shall walk side by side."

They moved through the halls together, Hattie clasping Senemut's arm protectively and looking everyone they passed in the eye. After a surprised glance or gasp, all averted their eyes and bowed, from the servants to the most exalted noble.

Let them stare! she thought. *I will not let them intimidate me any longer. I am pharaoh, for good or ill, and I must behave so.*

After a time she relaxed, enjoying the color returning to Senemut's cheeks and the life to his step.

As they approached the throne room, Hattie heard the sound of running feet behind them. A messenger appeared and flung himself at her feet, panting and sweating. "They have returned, Majesty," he gasped, and thrust a papyrus scroll at her.

"Thank you." She took the scroll, but paused before reading it. "It looks as if you have traveled a great distance. You may go to the palace kitchen and have the cooks feed you before you return to your post."

"I give you my thanks, Noble One," the messenger said, then turned and scurried away in the direction of the kitchen.

Hattie unrolled the scroll and scrutinized it. "Oh, Senemut!" she cried. "The expedition to Punt has returned safely. They will arrive in Thebes within the hour! Come...I must dress and make ready to receive them."

Senemut grinned. "I confess I am surprised they have returned. I should have trusted in you. You knew they would come back, did you not?" He straightened and started back in the direction of her rooms. "Come! We must hasten!"

Laughing, they hurried down the hall together, arm-in-arm.

Nesi worked her usual magic with Hattie's clothing and hair, and in less than an hour she and Senemut were in the throne room, ready to receive Chancellor Neshi. The room was crowded with nobles and priests, all eager to hear about the fabled land, and a festive air was evident. Servants moved through the crowd, dispensing goblets of wine and beer. Senemut stood behind Hattie's throne. She had tried to convince him to sit at her side, but to no avail.

"It is not suitable," was all he said.

She resolved to keep a close eye on him and if he looked tired, she would put a quick end to the audience.

Chancellor Neshi was announced. He strode into the room looking tired but sun-browned and fit, dressed in a clean white kilt, sandals and curled black wig. "Divine Majesty," he said, bowing low.

"Chancellor Neshi." Hattie inclined her head, then pointed to a stool at the foot of the dais. "Please be seated. You have had a long journey, and we wish to hear every detail!"

Neshi seated himself. "Thank you, Majesty. The journey was indeed long, but without peril—beyond the usual dangers of seasickness, spoiled food, confinement and boredom. We fell to our knees and praised Amun when we arrived safely and moored at Punt, Land of the God."

"Amun be praised," Hattie murmured in return.

"After mooring, we unloaded our trade goods onto small boats and made for the shore. There we found a small village and it was the most wondrous thing I have seen!" Neshi smiled broadly and gestured. "It was located in a crowd of immense trees that seemed to reach up to touch the sky. There were ebony, palm, and the sacred incense trees, and others I could not distinguish. I have never seen so many trees all in one place!"

Hattie wasn't surprised. There were few trees in the desert country of Egypt, where rain was scarce and water was in short supply.

"The dwellings of the villagers were shaped like beehives and set high on poles," Neshi continued. "They climb ladders to enter their homes each night. Defense is quite easy. All they do is pull up the ladders, and their homes are near impregnable. Playing in the trees surrounding the village were monkeys of every shape and size, while through the trees roamed animals of the most bizarre variety. We have brought some home for Your Majesty."

A ripple of wonder drifted through the crowd, and Hattie held up her hand for silence. "Please continue. Did you meet with the inhabitants of the village?"

"Aye, Majesty. I entered the village carrying my staff of office, accompanied by eight of our soldiers and their captain. We made an impressive display, I believe, since the villagers fled at the sight of us." He grinned. "But before long we were able to convince them of our peaceful intentions, and we were greeted by the King of Punt, one Parihu by name."

"Was he friendly? Did he wish to trade with Egypt?" Hattie asked.

"He was most anxious to do so," Neshi assured her.

His prompt cooperation was no doubt due to the numerous axes, spears and soldiers accompanying Neshi, Hattie thought, but said nothing.

"He had fine features, but masked them with a long beard." Neshi shuddered. All Egyptian men prided themselves on being clean-shaven. "He wore numerous gold rings on his left leg, from ankle to thigh, and a dagger in his belt. We were also greeted by Queen Ati. Highness, I know not if I can do justice to a description of the queen. She was of normal height, but of enormous girth." He spread his hands wide to indicate a grotesquely obese person. "Her costume was of the finest sheer fabric, which revealed and emphasized her unusual size. A small donkey carried her everywhere, as she was much too heavy to walk." Neshi shrugged. "She was judged to be most beautiful in the eyes of her subjects."

Laughter wafted through the room, and even Hattie found it difficult to keep a smile from her lips. In Egypt, slender and trim forms were considered the height of beauty and were practical as well in a country of such great heat. No doubt the Egyptian soldiers had never seen a person of Queen Ati's statuesque proportions before.

"We presented to His Majesty King Parihu beads, bracelets, axes, daggers, fine Egyptian linen, bronze and copper mirrors, bread, fruit, and casks of wine and beer," Neshi continued. "He, in turn, sent out a group of his best guides to lead our soldiers into the interior of Punt, to collect ebony and incense trees for Amun's temple.

"These and many other wonders we have brought back with us, for the glory of Amun and Your Majesty Maatkare." Neshi inclined his head to Hattie and she nodded. "Before we set sail home for Egypt, laden with the goods of Punt, we erected on the shore a fine granite statue of Your Majesty and your sacred father Amun, which will be worshiped by all the land. We journeyed north by sea in our treasure-laden ships to the port of Quseir, dismantled and carried the ships and cargo across the desert to the Nile at Coptos, then returned by sail to Thebes."

Hattie stood. "Chancellor Neshi, you have completed a most remarkable and difficult task, and surely won the favor of Amun as well as my praise and thanks. Never has any ruler been presented with such a bounty." She stripped a gold bracelet from each arm and held them out to him. "Please take these, as the first token of my gratitude. Be assured, there will be more."

Neshi went down on one knee to accept the bracelets. "Many thanks for your gift and your favor, Divine One. I live to serve you!" He rose and bowed. "Will Your Majesty accompany me now to the wharfs, so you may see for yourself all we have brought?"

"Of course!" Hattie turned to Senemut and eyed him appraisingly. He was still a bit pale, but he grinned at her, obviously savoring her triumph. "Come," she said, and held out her hand to him. "We will accompany Chancellor Neshi to the wharf."

She grasped Senemut's arm and they passed out of the throne room together in Neshi's wake.

* * *

Hattie, Senemut, and Neshi stood together on the wharf under a hastily erected canopy that provided some small relief from the stifling heat. Hattie had tried to convince Senemut to sit, but he refused to do so unless she sat as well, and Hattie was too excited to sit. The ships, riding low in the water from their enormous cargo of wealth from Punt, were being unloaded and the goods paraded along the street in the direction of the temple of Amun, where Hapuseneb waited to receive them and dedicate the finest of the items for the use of Amun. Crowds of onlookers jostled each other for position along the street and wharf to see the bounty that Amun's representatives had claimed in his name and the name of Hatshepsut and Egypt.

Hattie remembered the excitement she'd felt as a child, waiting for the Fourth of July parade to begin. She felt the same thrill now, anxious to see what Neshi and his ships had brought back from Punt. First to be unloaded were the sacred incense trees. Sailors struggled to carry the frankincense and myrrh trees, each planted in a basket and hung in a canvas sling between two long carrying poles. Some of them would be planted at the temple of Amun, while others would grace Hatshepsut's mortuary temple, *Djeser-Djeseru*, still under construction under the cliffs across the river from Thebes.

Next came men carrying long planks of ebony and cedar wood, boomerangs the Puntites used to hunt, enormous ivory elephant tusks, gold both in nugget form and in jewelry, containers filled with precious ointments, and blocks of resin. The resin and ointments, Senemut explained at Hattie's look of puzzlement, were used in the mummification process.

Then a group of sailors maneuvered a herd of small, short-horned cattle down the gangplank and into the street. For a moment, chaos reigned as the cattle bellowed and charged this way and that, confused by the milling crowds of people, the noise and unfamiliar sights and scents. At last the sweating, cursing sailors got them under control and drove them down the street in the direction of the temple.

Next out of the ship was a huge gray ape, the sacred animal of Thoth, the Egyptian god of wisdom. The ape wore a golden collar and leather leash and followed his single sailor guide meekly enough, though he bared his teeth at those onlookers who ventured too close, causing ripples of panic in the crowd.

"Oh, Senemut," Hattie said. "It is like a circus parade! What a wonderful sight."

"What is a circus, Majesty?" Senemut asked, frowning.

"It is held in a tent…there are many strange animals and performers…food is sold and parents bring their children to see…" She waved her arms helplessly. "I cannot describe it better. It is like a festival, I suppose."

Senemut nodded, then directed her attention back to the ships, his eyes wide. "Look! What is that animal they bring out now?"

Hattie clapped her hands. "It is a giraffe! Oh, Senemut, there are two of them! Are they not the loveliest creatures you have ever seen?"

"Lovely would not be my description," he retorted, one eyebrow raised. "They are most ungainly creatures. How does the food they eat manage to travel down that long neck and reach the stomach before they perish of hunger? And how do they reach the water when they are thirsty?"

"They must spread their legs and bow in a most clumsy manner to drink," she explained. "I have seen them do this in a zoo—"

"Zoo?" Neshi interrupted. "What is a zoo, Majesty?"

"A place where exotic animals are kept in cages so people may see them…" She stopped short at the blank looks on Neshi's and Senemut's faces. "*Ai*, never mind." She waved her hand to dismiss the idea and turned back to the ships. "Look, Senemut, it is a rhinoceros!"

He shook his head. "Another fanciful creature I would not have believed in had you described it to me. I suppose you have seen one of these also, in your zoo?"

Hattie nodded. "As I recall, visitors to the zoo had to stay well back from the wall around the rhinoceros's enclosure. It seems they tend to…ah…" She blushed. "They urinate to mark their territory, and they liked to do so in the direction of the wall."

Neshi grinned. "Then mayhap that explains the haste the people are making to remove themselves from the vicinity of the creature." He gestured toward the street leading to the temple, and indeed, Hattie saw a wave of movement away from the street as the rhinoceros was led through the crowd.

Next came bales of panther and leopard skins, followed quickly by a snarling black panther led by several very nervous-looking sailors, each holding a leather leash fastened to a gold collar around the animal's neck. The panther's sleek dark fur shone in the hot , and his sharp fangs gleamed. The crowd fell back in earnest at his approach and he was dragged, growling and protesting, toward the temple.

A troop of chattering, shrieking monkeys emerged from the hold of one of the ships and they, too, were safely herded in the direction of the temple at the end of long leashes. A wave of childish laughter followed in their wake.

"I confess I am glad to see the last of those creatures," Neshi said. "They are like an undisciplined bunch of children given free rein to run about and behave as they choose. I look forward to my first good sleep tonight, without the sounds of their mayhem to wake me!" He sighed in exaggerated relief, and Senemut laughed.

Last to emerge was a straggly, weary group of seven male Puntites. "Oh, Neshi," Hattie cried. "Who are they?"

"They are the emissaries of the King of Punt, sent to greet you in his name, Majesty," Neshi replied.

"Why did you not let them disembark first? It must be blisteringly hot on those ships."

"Majesty, the goods dedicated to the service of Amun take precedence over the comfort of foreigners," he replied, looking surprised.

Hattie shook her head but declined to engage in any further useless discussion. She clapped her hands, and a servant appeared almost at once. "See to it that my guests—" She gestured at the ambassadors. "—are escorted to my palace at once. Give them food and drink, and they will surely wish a bath. Then they are to rest undisturbed until tomorrow, when I will meet with them." The servant bowed and hastened away to do her bidding.

She turned again to Neshi. "You have done a wonderful job, Neshi, and I will see that you are suitably rewarded with land and with honors. I am very pleased!"

Neshi bowed. "I will serve Your Majesty faithfully as long as I live."

* * *

"I fear the gods are protecting her, as you have said," Snefru muttered. "Mayhap we err in trying to rid Egypt of her. I have no wish to be struck down by the gods."

"*Ast!*" Hapuseneb said irritably as they watched the endless, weary procession of Punt goods flow into the courtyard of the temple of Amun. "She has been lucky, I grant you, but nothing more. I do not believe that Amun wishes a woman on the throne, or he would have placed one there before now." *And I certainly cannot allow a woman to remain on the throne, especially such a strong-minded one.*

"I am not so certain—" Snefru began.

"Well, *I* am certain," Hapuseneb cut in, glaring at him. "Am I not the High Priest of Amun? Who are you to question me?"

Snefru's face contorted into a belligerent frown, then smoothed out almost at once and settled into his usual expression of indifference. "Forgive me, old friend. I grow cautious and timid in my old age. I believe you, for if you know not the will of Amun, then who does? And truly, if Amun were angry at our meddling, would he not have struck us down long since?"

Hapuseneb nodded, relieved at passing through yet another crisis safely with the impulsive general. "You are right. Sometimes I think we are nothing but playthings for the gods. They throw us down like the painted sticks in a game of *sennet*, and wait to see which of us will emerge victorious. Well, Hatshepsut shall not triumph over me! If it takes my lifetime, I will see her cast down from her throne and Tuthmosis ruling in her stead, assisted by his most loyal retainers." He gestured at the panther being pulled into the temple. "It will just take us a bit longer now. But never fear. We will prevail. Of that I have no doubt."

Eying the bounty of Punt spread out in the courtyard, Snefru scowled. "May the gods make it so, for this triumph of hers will only strengthen the love of the common people for her. And once aroused from their usual torpor, the commoners are a force to be reckoned with."

"I have no intention of striking at her openly," Hapuseneb retorted. "We spoke of magic, did we not?"

Snefru nodded. "Aye, we did. Have you hit upon the right spell to serve our needs?"

"I think so. Hatshepsut is cunning, but she is a woman, and all women are easily lured by the sight of gold and jewels." Hapuseneb rubbed his hands together. He hadn't intended to discuss his plan in detail with Snefru, but Hatshepsut's unexpected triumph in Punt had stung him severely. Praise, even from a fool, would soothe him. "I have had fashioned a most wonderful golden pectoral necklace with a central figure of Horus, encrusted with jewels. I shall present it to her myself. Hatshepsut will not be able to resist the combined seduction of gold and of Horus, which bolsters her claim to the throne. And when she touches it..." He paused dramatically.

"Aye?" Snefru said, impatience warring with dread in his expression.

Hapuseneb grinned like a toothy shark. "When she touches it, the magic spell I shall cast upon it will take hold, and she will disappear from our lives and from Egypt forever."

CHAPTER 24

Back in her apartment in Chicago, Hattie was soaking in a warm bubble bath, a glass of chilled white wine on a low table next to the tub, soft jazz wafting in from the radio in the living room. A warm, fluffy towel and plush bathrobe awaited her, then a ticket to the orchestra concert. Her life was as it had always been, yet tears streamed down her cheeks and her chest ached from sobbing. She had never felt so alone. She was back home at last, so why did it seem empty and meaningless? Why did her heart ache as if it held a wound from which she'd never recover?

She heard a small sound and turned toward the open bathroom door. Her jaw dropped as the figure of Hatshepsut materialized in all her ethereal beauty. "You!" Hattie breathed. "You did this to me, did you not?"

Hatshepsut nodded. "You are almost finished with your task. When it is completed, I shall resume my life and you shall return here to your home. Is that not what you have wished for?"

"Aye. Nay. I mean…" Hattie floundered for words. "I thought I wanted to return home. But I cannot leave Senemut! Wherever he is, *there* is my home. Without him, my life is barren and lonely."

Hatshepsut smiled tenderly. "Then you have learned a great lesson, have you not? Home and hearth mean nothing without love to warm them."

"So you will let me stay with him?" Hattie asked eagerly. "You will not send me back to Chicago?"

"Oh, nay. I am afraid you must return here, to your home. Once I resume my life, there is no other place for you to go. Your spirit must have a body to inhabit, or it will flee to the afterlife.

Surely, that is not what you wish?"

Hattie frowned, and then slowly shook her head. "Nay, I do not wish to die. But I cannot live without Senemut. I love him. How am I to go on without him? Please, you must help me!"

"Mayhap there is something I can do. I am not certain." Hatshepsut paused. "You are sure you wish this?"

Hattie nodded emphatically. "I am positive."

"Very well. This I promise—I will do all I can to see that you and Senemut will be together, though I know not if my powers extend that far. But I warn you…there will be heartbreak first. I cannot prevent it." Hatshepsut's image shimmered and grew transparent.

"Wait!" Hattie cried. "What do you mean, there will be heartbreak first?"

But it was too late. Hatshepsut had vanished.

* * *

"Hattie!"

Someone was shaking her shoulder. She didn't want to wake up, but the shaker was most persistent. At last, she opened her eyes grudgingly and saw Senemut leaning over her, a look of concern etched across his face. She smiled up at him, and he relaxed. "Why did you wake me? It is nowhere near dawn."

"You were crying out in your sleep as if the demons of Set were pursuing you." He dropped a kiss onto her forehead. "I would not see you suffer so, even in dreams."

She leaned back into his arms and moaned as she recalled the fading images of her nightmare. "It was much worse than Set. I had returned to my own time, but I was alone there. I have never felt so bereft! May it please Amun to allow me to stay with you for all my life." She shuddered.

"Do not fear, little one," Senemut murmured in her ear as he stroked her hair. "It will take more than a dream to tear me from your side. This I promise."

This I promise. Why did that sound so familiar? A sudden sense of dread washed over her. "Senemut, I am afraid…something is to happen to us, and I know not what. But it will be terrible and there is naught I can do to prevent it."

"Shh, nothing will happen to us. You are still frightened because of the images in your sleep. We are safe." He kissed her again, this time on the lips. "Mayhap I know a way to make you forget your worry."

"Aye, Senemut," she whispered. "Please, help me forget."

Senemut rolled over, covering her body with his. "My love," he breathed, claiming her lips again.

Fire leapt through her veins as she returned his kiss.

Suddenly, the curtain flew aside and a dark figure darted into the room. "Watch out!" Hattie gasped, her voice muffled against his shoulder.

Senemut tried to rise, but the figure was already at her bedside. She saw the intruder's arm rise and fall savagely, and heard Senemut groan as he slumped down on top of her. "Senemut!" she cried. "Senemut, are you all right?"

There was no response. He lay sprawled across her, a dead weight. The attacker disappeared as quickly as he had arrived.

"Guards!" she screamed. She put her arms around Senemut and rolled him onto his back, wriggling out from under him as she did so. She felt a patch of wetness on her chest and stomach. Was it his blood? Where were the guards? She needed help and she needed light!

At last, two guards appeared with torches in their hands. "May we assist you, Majesty?"

"Someone has attacked Lord Senemut. Find the assassin at once, or I will have your heads," she snapped. "Give me one of those torches. And send Nesi to me. Go!"

"Aye, Your Majesty," they stammered in unison, turning pale under their tans, and hastened to do her bidding.

Hattie stuck the torch in a wall bracket over her bed and examined Senemut more closely. Blood was everywhere and it seemed to be spreading out from underneath him. Gently, she rolled him onto his side and leaned over to examine his back. She gasped as she saw a gaping stab wound to the right of his spine, just above his waist. Blood pumped from the laceration and she knew his life force was ebbing with each spurt. Seizing the linen sheet, she wadded it up and pressed it against the wound, but it seemed to be to no avail. Blood quickly soaked through the sheet and flowed between her outspread fingers.

"Senemut, you cannot die. You cannot! How am I to live without you? Please, open your eyes, Senemut. Speak to me," she begged.

His eyelids fluttered open for a minute and his lips moved as he struggled to focus on her.

"What is it, Senemut?" She leaned closer, watching his face intently.

"I…I love you, Hattie," he whispered. "I am sorry…" His eyes rolled back in his head and he slumped against her.

"Nay, Senemut," Hattie sobbed, shaking him. "Do not leave me, please!" But her heart felt as empty as it had in her nightmare, and she knew that this time, Senemut was gone.

* * *

Hapuseneb grunted with satisfaction as he straightened from bending over a worktable in a tiny, torchlit room in the secret innermost reaches of the temple of Amun. "So, the usurper is dead at last, is he?"

"Aye, so he is," Snefru said, rubbing his hands together. "And high time! He has been more difficult to dispatch than a wily jackal. The hired assassin has been silenced and his body dumped in the Nile. No one will trace him to us…if his remains are ever found." He grinned. "I believe the crocodiles will be of great assistance there."

"Good! Then it is only a matter of time before we are rid of Hatshepsut also," Hapuseneb said.

"I have taken care of my part of our arrangement," Snefru continued. "What about you? Are you finished with the spell for the necklace?"

"I am just beginning. Would you care to assist me?" Hapuseneb beckoned to him, reveling in the look of sheer terror that crossed Snefru's face.

Snefru held up his hands and backed away. "Nay, I would not. I have never dabbled in black magic, and I do not intend to start now. I will not take the risk of angering the gods and having them send out their *khefts* to steal my soul." He stumbled and nearly fell over a small stool. Righting it, he stammered, "I will take my leave now. I wish you success in your venture." He turned and fled the room.

Hapuseneb chuckled. "Snefru, you were ever fearful of powers you cannot see and touch. Fortunately, I have no such apprehensions." He returned his attention to the necklace spread on the table.

It was a fine piece of craftsmanship, and unfortunate indeed that the maker had met with a fatal "accident". A golden falcon formed the central portion of the pectoral necklace, the symbol of pharaoh's authority to rule over Egypt and his protection by the falcon-god Horus. The falcon's outspread wings were resplendent with beads of turquoise, lapis lazuli, gold and colored glass, glittering even in the weak torchlight. The piercing green jasper eyes seemed strangely alive.

Hapuseneb had dictated the hieroglyphics to be inscribed on the body of the bird to a scribe, whose journey to the afterlife had also regrettably been hastened. The hieroglyphics represented a prayer to protect the life of pharaoh; only Hapuseneb knew the prayer was offered for the life of Tuthmosis, not Hatshepsut. Now, all he had to do was cast the spell on the thing, and it could be presented to Hatshepsut and send her to her doom.

First, he burned a pinch of incense in a small pottery bowl with a lotus flower motif and raised it over his head. "Hear me, Maat, goddess of justice and truth. It is I, Hapuseneb, High Priest of Amun, who calls. May my words be pleasing to your ears, as this incense is pleasing to your nostrils," he chanted, as the sweet smoke rose and curled to the ceiling. The flickering torch threw grotesque shadows of Hapuseneb's uplifted arms on the walls.

He set down the bowl and lifted the necklace, passed it back and forth through the incense smoke seven times, then raised it toward the ceiling. "Oh, Maat, I ask you to imbue this golden necklace with your power. Let Hatshepsut be taken far from Egypt when she touches it. Let her be toppled from the throne of Horus and thrust into the darkness beyond the grave. No female should be allowed to rule all of Egypt—let her reap the reward she so richly deserves. Let there be *maat* in the land of Egypt again."

A ferocious wind arose and swept through the room. The torch sputtered and went out. "It shall be as you desire, Hapuseneb, High Priest of Amun," a spectral voice howled, coming from everywhere and nowhere. "Hatshepsut shall receive justice, *maat* shall be restored, and you shall receive what you deserve as well."

"Thank you, Maat, goddess of truth," Hapuseneb cried above the roar of the wind, dropping the necklace and flinging himself prostrate to the ground. "May your name ever be praised!"

As quickly as it began, the wind stopped. Hapuseneb arose cautiously, straightened his robe, and retrieved the necklace. He had a gift to present.

CHAPTER 25

Hattie pushed away the tray of food that Nesi had set before her. "Take it away, Nesi. I have no appetite."

"But, Majesty," her servant protested, "you have eaten nothing in three days, nor have you slept! You must eat and you must rest, else you will fall ill."

"I care not whether I live or die," Hattie murmured. She was only mildly surprised to discover that her words were true. She had lost Senemut and, with him, her enthusiasm and energy for life. She no longer cared if she completed her mission, if she returned to her own time. She had nothing left here, and nothing awaited her in the twenty-first century. "My survival means nothing to me when I have lost the only man I have ever loved."

Nesi clucked sympathetically. "Aye, Your Majesty. But Lord Senemut would not want you to grieve so, I know it. He was ever a kind man and you were his first concern. Surely, you can eat something for his sake?"

Hattie eyed the servant suspiciously. Nesi bravely returned her stare, refusing to drop her eyes.

"You are becoming much too smart for me," Hattie said at last and sighed. It was easier to give in than to argue with the girl, for she had no strength to quarrel. "Aye, very well, leave the food. I shall try to eat a little."

"Amun be praised! Thank you, Majesty. And a small nap would do you good." A smile lit Nesi's face. "I will be outside if you require anything else."

Hattie took a bite of bread. It tasted like dust in her mouth. Absently, she crumbled the rest. Why had she come to this accursed time and place, only to have her heart broken? Surely Hatshepsut could have found someone else to carry on her mission who would have handled things properly, leaving Hattie free to stay in her own time with her heart untouched. She curled up on the bed, clutching one of Senemut's cloaks to her chest.

"Oh, Senemut," she whispered. "Why did you leave me, alone and friendless? What will I do without you? How shall I go on?"

At last, exhaustion and stress overcame her, and she dropped off into a fitful slumber.

It seemed she had only been asleep an instant when she felt someone shake her. Opening her eyes a slit, Hattie saw Nesi bending over her.

"Forgive me, Majesty, but there was no other way to wake you," Nesi said. "You did not answer when I called to you."

Hattie sighed and rubbed her burning eyes, then pushed herself upright. "Do not worry. I am not angry. What do you want?"

"There is a messenger waiting to see you." The servant glanced over her shoulder and made the sign of the sacred eye of Horus. "Majesty, he is from the House of the Dead," she whispered.

"The House of the Dead? Nay, send him away. I do not wish to hear any details of the mummification process." Hattie shuddered.

"But, Majesty," Nesi said, looking again over her shoulder, "the messenger says it is most urgent. He carries a message from the Ka priest at the house of embalming."

Hattie swallowed convulsively as the bite of bread she had swallowed earlier threatened to come up. "Very well...very well. Send him in."

A tall, gangly priest with a shaved head, dressed in a coarse linen kilt, entered and bowed deeply. "I am sorry to interrupt you, Majesty, but I have news I fear you will not like."

"Nothing could be worse than what I have already endured," Hattie mumbled. Then she sighed. "Come, give me your news."

"Radiant One, I know not how to explain it…but…may Amun forgive us, the body of Lord Senemut has disappeared." He gasped the final words in a rush, then dropped to his knees and prostrated himself on the floor at her feet.

Hattie frowned. "Disappeared? What do you mean, Senemut's body has disappeared?"

The priest glanced up at her from the floor. "Lord Senemut was brought to us three days ago after his…his unfortunate accident. It was late in the day, Majesty, so we merely covered his body—with the finest of linen sheets, of course. When we returned to the house of embalming the following morning…" He abased himself again. "Majesty, Lord Senemut's body was gone. The sheet lay on the embalming table undisturbed, as if no one had ever touched it. But Lord Senemut had vanished."

Hattie shook her head, only succeeding in making it pound. "Have you searched? Surely, he has just been moved to another part of the facility."

"Aye, Royal One," the priest said. "We have searched from one end of the building to the other these two days past, but we can find no trace of him." His voice sank to a whisper. "It is said that a mighty wind arose in that quarter of the city that night. Some say it was caused by the wings of Horus, arriving to take Lord Senemut bodily to the afterlife."

"I do not think that is the case," Hattie said, scowling.

"I can offer you no other explanation," the priest stammered. "I am sorry, Majesty. I stand ready to accept any punishment you decree." He quivered, but held his position at her feet.

Hattie's eyes cleared momentarily from the mist of grief she'd been in since Senemut's death. A brave man lay before her, ready to accept death if she should order it so, for something he hadn't done. "Do not fear. I do not hold you or your workers responsible, and I will not punish you."

The priest looked up cautiously. "I…I thank you, Divine One. You are most merciful!"

The pall of despair dropped over Hattie again. "It matters not what has happened to the body. Lord Senemut is gone.

That is all that matters to me." She gestured at the priest and he hurried out, bowing all the way.

Hattie dropped down onto her bed, clutching Senemut's cloak to her. "It matters not…nothing matters now. My love, and my life, is gone."

* * *

Hours later, Hattie still lay curled up on her bed, her eyes burning, her soul temporarily depleted of tears and grief. Nesi carefully poked her head into the room. "Majesty?"

"Aye, Nesi?" Her voice sounded pained and dry, even to her.

"Hapuseneb, the high priest of Amun, is here to see you. Shall I admit him?"

Hattie sighed and pushed herself upright. "All right. Send him in." She pushed a shaky hand through her tousled hair and made a halfhearted attempt to straighten her gown.

Hapuseneb entered and bowed, his hands behind his back. "Majesty, forgive me for intruding on your sorrow. I know your heart is burdened and your spirit oppressed."

"Thank you for your sympathy, Hapuseneb," she said, rising tiredly from the bed.

"How are the young prince and princess taking the news?" He paced back and forth, glancing at her occasionally, but never turning his back.

"Tuthmosis is away, training with the army, as you know," Hattie said, frowning. She was mildly intrigued by Hapuseneb's behavior since he had never before shown any concern for her. "I have sent him a messenger bearing the news. Neferure is heartbroken, as you may well imagine. Senemut was her first tutor and she loved him well." Hattie sighed and massaged her temples. "I cannot comfort her, nor can she comfort me."

"It is regrettable," he murmured, darting another glance at her and then looking away.

"Aye. It is." She paused, but he didn't respond. "Is that all you came to say, or do you wish something from me?"

Hapuseneb opened his mouth and closed it, then tried again. "I…forgive me for my audacity, Majesty, but I have brought you a gift. I think it will help to lighten your heart." He brought out his hands from behind his back at last and thrust at her a beautifully decorated, small cedar box. "I pray you will accept this poor token of my esteem."

"Why, Hapuseneb! I am surprised." Hattie allowed her expression to soften. Perhaps she had misjudged him. If he could offer her sympathy in her time of grief, he couldn't be all bad. "It is very kind of you, and I thank you." She reached out for the box and Hapuseneb placed it in her hands, an odd smile playing about the corners of his mouth.

Hattie ran her fingers over the exquisite carving on the lid, then opened the box. It was deep and dark, revealing nothing of its interior. Caring little whether it was a piece of jewelry or a poisonous snake, she plunged her hand into the box and pulled out its contents. Her jaw dropped as she saw what dangled from her trembling fingers. It was the golden pectoral necklace that had brought her to Egypt, the eye of Horus glittering in the dim light. Confused, she turned to Hapuseneb. "What is this…where did you get…"

A wicked grin split his face. "I have rid Egypt of the usurper Senemut, and now I shall rid her of you, too!"

An electric shock pulsed through Hattie's hand and up her arm. She tried to let go of the necklace, but she couldn't seem to loosen her grip on it. Her legs buckled and gave out, and she dropped to the bed.

"Why?" she whispered, as waves of dizziness assaulted her. She should be happy to be returning to her own home at last. Wasn't that what she had worked for all this time? Hadn't she turned the palace upside down searching for the necklace, and tried to find a magic spell or charm to aid her? Why, then, was she frightened now that her goal was at last at hand?

Realization suddenly dawned that home was no longer Chicago…it was Egypt. She belonged here, as she had never belonged in Chicago.

"Because you are a meddler. Because you are a *woman*, and have no place on the throne of Egypt." Hapuseneb sneered. "And because the boy will be more easily controlled than you. Egypt will founder under your rule. We need a warrior king on the throne. And I intend to fashion that warrior king."

The scent of incense burned strong in Hattie's nostrils and her vision blurred. "So, it was you all along?" she whispered, struggling to hold onto consciousness.

"Aye, it was me," he hissed. "Snefru dispatched your precious Senemut, but I claim credit for finally ridding Egypt of you. My name will live forever!"

Hattie's vision grew black around the edges before all sight disappeared. Hapuseneb's evil grin was the final thing she saw. She was falling, falling into a deep, dark pit with no one to catch her, no one to help her. She was all alone.

Suddenly, she felt the same cooling sense of comfort she'd experienced when she passed out in the museum after touching the necklace. Turning, she saw the lovely, slender woman she knew at last was the real Hatshepsut, not just a figment of her imagination. "You!" she breathed.

"Aye. You have performed the task I set you, and I am most grateful. Tuthmosis is safe and will live to rule Egypt. I know now who the traitors are, and do not fear, they will be punished." The queen frowned. "When I was poisoned by Hapuseneb, my powers were not sufficiently strong, in my illness, to allow me to purge my body of the venom and also keep my *ka* intact. All I could do was search down through the millennia, bodiless, for one who could perform my task and make my body habitable again. My blood runs true in your veins. You were the perfect choice."

"I am glad I could help you. You say we are kin and I believe you now, for Egypt seems as much a part of me as my own flesh."

"That is as it should be," Hatshepsut said. "Yet you have gone further than I asked. You have also loved and protected my beloved daughter Neferure. I thank you for that with all my heart. Now you can take up the threads of your own life again and be happy."

Hattie sighed. "But it is too late for me to be happy…too late. Senemut is gone."

Hatshepsut smiled enigmatically. "Possibly."

Hattie opened her eyes wide. "What do you mean, possibly?" Hatshepsut shrugged. "I must return to my body now, else my *ka* will be lost in the void forever. You will understand soon… this I promise." She held up her hand in blessing. "In a moment, you will return to your own life. But know that my immeasurable gratitude goes with you." She faded away, leaving Hattie alone in the darkness.

But not for long. Glowing in the dark, like an image on a distant movie screen, Hattie saw Hatshepsut lying lifeless on her bed in the palace at Thebes. Hapuseneb leaned over her, holding a small mirror under her nostrils to check for the breath of life.

Hatshepsut's gown suddenly shivered as if stirred by a violent wind. Her chest rose sharply and she sprang upright, knocking the mirror from Hapuseneb's hand. He stumbled backward and fell to the floor. "Majesty!" he stammered. "Majesty, I thought you were…"

"Guards!" Hatshepsut cried. "Come to me at once!"

The curtain flew aside and two burly guards rushed in.

"Arrest him," she ordered, pointing. "Arrest Hapuseneb! He has tried to murder me."

"But I thought you had…" Hapuseneb sputtered. "I did nothing, I swear…"

"Be silent, traitor," Hatshepsut ordered. "Take him out of my sight, and see that he does not escape. Send a message to the army and have General Snefru arrested, too. He is a member of this conspiracy and is behind the murder of Lord Senemut. Bind the assassins and cast them off the peak of the Temple of Amun, and feed their bodies to the crocodiles so that all may see how Egypt deals with treason and treachery. Go!"

The guards saluted her, then dragged the still-protesting Hapuseneb away.

The scene dimmed and Hattie found herself alone again in the dark. The dizziness returned. She fell to the ground and knew no more.

CHAPTER 26

Consciousness returned slowly to Hattie. Her head ached abominably. She was lying on a cold, hard floor. She opened her eyes a slit. The worktable and file cabinets of the storage room at the museum swam into view. Was her sojourn in ancient Egypt merely a dream, then? Had she hallucinated it all during a period of oblivion brought on by the blow to her head when she fell?

No, it couldn't be a dream, she thought, as she squeezed her eyes shut. She recalled every detail of her time in Egypt—the battle with the Nubians, her coronation, the assassination attempts against her. She could smell the incense and lotus blossoms, taste the honey cakes and date wine. Surely, she couldn't dream such richness and detail, could she? She saw Senemut's handsome features before her; she felt his warm lips on hers, his gentle hands caressing her. Her heart ached fiercely at the loss of him. Could she imagine such pain, such profound sorrow?

"Hattie? Can you hear me? Are you all right?"

The voice sounded familiar. Hattie opened her eyes again and saw Tom bending over her.

"Thank goodness," he exclaimed. "What happened? Oh, I never should've left you alone."

"It's…it's all right," she whispered. "It was my fault. I touched the necklace and then something happened. I got dizzy…I'm not sure why…and I fell." She touched the back of her head gingerly and winced. "I hit my head on the table. I must've passed out."

"You may have a concussion. Don't move," Tom urged. "Just lie back. I've called the paramedics and they should be here any minute."

"I don't need the paramedics. I'm fine." She tried to rise, but lightheadedness assailed her and she lay back.

"Now, you see? I told you not to move." He patted her shoulder comfortingly.

"What…what time is it?" she whispered. "How long have I been here?"

"I left you here two hours ago. I should've stayed with you! I hope you'll forgive—" Tom turned at the sound of approaching footsteps. "That must be them. Stay still, will you? I'll be right back."

Only two hours? She had lived a lifetime in that short period. Hattie groaned, but made no further attempt to sit up. *I have no reason to hurry home*, she thought. *No one waits for me. I've lost Senemut and all that I hold dear.*

"Can you speak to me? Do you know your name?"

The voice was male, but it wasn't Tom. A paramedic in a white uniform leaned over her. The sound of another voice drifted back to her…*Are you all right, Majesty? Do you know your name?* A tear ran down her cheek. "My…my name is Hattie," she whispered, a knife cleaving her heart in two. "Hattie Williams, from Chicago."

"Very good," the man said brusquely. "How many fingers am I holding up?"

"Three."

"Can you tell me what happened?" he asked, taking her pulse as he spoke.

She shrugged. "I had some kind of a dizzy spell and I fell. I must've hit my head on the table. That's all I remember." *That's all I'm going to tell you, anyway*, she added silently. *I don't want to be carted off to the funny farm.*

After endless questions and tests, the paramedic announced she should spend the night in the hospital "for observation".

"Oh no," Hattie protested, taking an interest in the proceedings for the first time. "I'm not going to the hospital. I want to go home."

"You've had a head injury. Twenty-four hours of observation is the usual procedure in these cases," the paramedic said stiffly.

"Well, call me unusual then," Hattie snapped. "I'm going home."

The man frowned. "Of course, I can't force you to check into the hospital. I can only urge you to do so. Do you have someone to stay with you? Someone should wake you every two hours to make sure you're not unconscious."

She shook her head.

"Do you at least have someone to drive you home?" he persisted. "You can't drive yourself. It isn't safe."

"I'll take a taxi," she murmured. *I have no one. I have no one*, thrummed through her head.

"I'll drive you home," Tom said. "And I'll stay the night. You need someone to look after you."

"No, you don't have to—"

Tom held up his hand to cut short her protest. "I insist. It's the least I can do! I feel guilty enough about this whole thing."

Hattie sighed. "All right. I don't have the energy to fight you about it. Thanks, Tom."

He grinned. "My pleasure. Ready to go home, lady? Your taxi's here." He helped her to her feet and ushered her and the ambulance crew out the door, closing and locking it behind him.

Hattie followed him to his car, steeling herself to avoid backward glances. Her life with Senemut was over. She had to accept that and move on. Somehow.

* * *

The phone rang and jolted Hattie out of a daydream of gliding down the Nile on the *Avenging Falcon* with Senemut, the sun glinting on his bronzed body, his face lit up with a smile as he told her tales of pharaohs and slaves, priests and courtiers. *Great Amun*, she thought irritably, *when will I get over this?*

She picked up the receiver. "Hello?"

"Hello, Hattie, it's Tom. How are you feeling today?"

"Swell," she replied wearily.

"Are you up to a visitor?"

"A visitor?" She shook her head. "Tom, you've been over here every day for the past week since I fell and hit my head in the storage room. My refrigerator is full of chicken soup, and my apartment is so clean, it glows. You don't need to visit me every day. I'm fine, really."

He laughed. "All right, I admit I've been a bit of a mother hen. But in addition to being your friend, I'm also your employer—and I want my most valuable employee back on the job! The deadline for the Hatshepsut book is breathing down my neck, and I need those drawings from you."

Hattie's eyes watered and she squeezed them shut, trying hard not to cry. "I'm sorry, Tom. I just haven't felt up to doing any work since my accident. But I'll try to get back to them today and finish them for you." She sighed. "I know you could've hired another artist to complete them, and I appreciate your patience."

"I don't want another artist. I want *you*," Tom insisted. "I have an idea for something that might help you get back in the swing of the project."

"Not another necklace. Please," she said, massaging her temples. She couldn't endure another reminder of all she'd lost.

"Oh no, it's nothing like that," he protested. "I have someone I'd like you to meet."

"Who?"

"His name is Sam Steward. He's an architect, and has been living and working in Egypt for many years. He's very familiar with Hatshepsut's temple and her other monuments. I think he can help you get a handle on her. What do you say? Shall I send him over?"

Hattie shrugged. "I don't care. You can if you like."

Tom was silent for a moment. "I wish you'd get your old enthusiasm back," he said at last. "Something's changed about you ever since your accident. You're like a ghost of yourself. Frankly, I miss the old Hattie."

"I do, too," she murmured. Then she shook herself. It wasn't fair to let Tom down. It wasn't his fault her life was meaningless now. "I'll try. Send him over. What was his name again…Sam?"

"Yes. I'll send him right over. He should be there within the hour. Thanks, Hattie!"

"You're welcome, Tom. 'Bye." She hung up and dropped back onto the sofa. This architect could come if he wished—it made no difference. She would finish the drawings as a favor to Tom. And then she'd never write, read, or speak the name of Hatshepsut again.

* * *

An hour later, her doorbell sounded. "Yes?" she called through the door without opening it.

"I am here to see Hattie Williams. My name is Sam Steward," came a warm male voice. He had a subtle, exotic accent, and though the language was English, she thought she recognized the voice. Her heart thudded to a stop. Could it be? Did she dare risk heartbreak again to find out?

Slowly, reluctantly, she opened the door with trembling hands. Her jaw dropped and she lifted her hand to her throat, staggering back a pace.

His long, dark hair didn't obscure his handsome face, and the jeans, t-shirt and denim jacket he wore only accentuated his well-muscled form. "Hattie?" he whispered, reaching out to her and smiling a familiar smile.

"No—no, it can't be," she whimpered, backing into the living room. "Senemut is dead! I can't endure this pain again. Please, go and leave me alone with my grief." She bumped into the couch and sat down abruptly.

He hurried to her and, dropping down on one knee, seized her hand. "It is I, little warrior. I am Senemut!"

Little warrior. Her breath caught in her throat. "You can't be… how can this be…I don't believe you!" She shook off his hand and stood, trying to work her way around him. She didn't know what kind of trick he was playing, but she had to get away from him or she'd lose her mind. "What kind of an evil game are you playing? You get out or…or I'll call the police!"

"Hattie." He shook his head sorrowfully as he rose and stood in front of her. "I understand your confusion. I, too, was confused when you told me you had traveled to Egypt from the future. But you must accept my story, as I accepted yours." He stood and reached into his inner jacket pocket. "Here is the proof you gave me of your journey through time. Now I return it to you as my proof."

Trembling, her heart pounding furiously, Hattie removed the tissue paper folded carefully around a thin, fragile piece of papyrus, and saw an image of her own face staring up at her. It was the drawing she'd made for Senemut, to show him what she truly looked like.

She raised her eyes to his as warm tears flooded down her cheeks. "Senemut, it *is* you!" she cried.

He smiled and nodded, then winked at her. "Aye, it is," he murmured, sweeping her into his arms. "I have been waiting an eternity for you, my love. What took you so long?"

AUTHOR'S NOTE

The principal Egyptian characters in *Lady of the Two Lands*—Hatshepsut, Senemut, Tuthmosis, Hapuseneb, Snefru, Neshi, Senimen—are historical figures. Secondary Egyptian characters and those of the twenty-first century are fictional, with names authentic to the period. Historical details of everyday life in ancient Egypt have been researched meticulously for accuracy. The time-travel aspect of the story is fictional (as far as I know), and I have taken artistic license in some details; for example, the length of time it took to build Hatshepsut's temple. Spelling of ancient Egyptian words and names is problematic since the vowels were often left to be filled in by the reader, so I chose spellings that seemed easiest for the English-speaking reader to pronounce.

Hatshepsut's and Senemut's bodies have never been found, and many of Hatshepsut's monuments and inscriptions were erased or destroyed by her successor, Tuthmosis III, so there is little to tell us how her reign ended or what became of Senemut, who predeceased Hatshepsut by a number of years. We do know that her reign was extraordinarily peaceful and prosperous, and she ruled Egypt for about twenty years.

For those who are interested, I consulted a number of sources:

Egypt: Land of the Pharaohs, Time-Life Books, 1992.

Gardiner, Alan H. *The Coronation of King Haremhab. The Journal of Egyptian Archaeology*, Vol. 39, 1953.

Gore, Rick. *Pharaohs of the Sun. National Geographic*, Vol. 199. No. 4, April 2001.

Shaw, Ian, ed., *The Oxford History of Ancient Egypt*, Oxford University Press, 2000.

Tyldesley, Joyce. *Hatchepsut: The Female Pharaoh*, Viking, 1996.

Tyldesley, Joyce. *Daughters of Isis: Women of Ancient Egypt*, Penguin Books, 1994.

Weeks, Kent R. *Valley of the Kings. National Geographic*, Vol, 194, No. 3, Sept. 1998.

What Life Was Like on the Banks of the Nile: Egypt 3050-30 B.C., Time-Life Books, 1997.

ABOUT ELIZABETH DELISI

Elizabeth Delisi wanted to be a writer since she was in first grade, and probably would have written in the womb if she could have convinced her mother to swallow a pencil.

Elizabeth is a multi-published, award-winning author of romance, mystery and suspense. She is also an instructor for Writer's Digest University, has taught Creative Writing at the community college level, has worked as a copyeditor for several small publishers, and edits for individuals. She holds a B.A. in English with a Creative Writing major from St. Leo University.

Elizabeth is currently at work on Deadly Destiny and Perilous Prediction, the sequels to Fatal Fortune.

Elizabeth lives in New Hampshire with her husband and feisty parakeet. She enjoys hearing from her readers.

GET IN TOUCH WITH ELIZABETH

Elizabeth Delisi
www.elizabethdelisi.com

Facebook
www.facebook.com/elizabeth.delisi

Twitter
twitter.com/delisi

Blog
www.elizabethdelisi.blogspot.com

Tirgearr Publishing
www.tirgearrpublishing.com/authors/Delisi_Elizabeth

BOOKS BY ELIZABETH

LOTTIE BALDWIN MYSTERIES

FATAL FORTUNE, #1
Released: June 2012
ISBN: 9781476498409

No one in Cheyenne, ND believes in Lottie Baldwin's psychic abilities; especially not Harlan Erikson, Lottie's boyfriend, and Chief Deputy in the Sheriff's Office. When a friend's husband disappears, Lottie can't leave it to Harlan. Armed with her courage and her tarot cards, she tries to solve the mystery herself, regardless of who attempts to stop her: Harlan, her friend—or the criminal.

OBSERVANT ORACLE, #2
Released: September 2015
ISBN: 9781310787782

Who murdered the Cheyenne State University student? Can deputy sheriff Harlan Erikson solve the case quickly enough to keep his fiancée, impulsive psychic Lottie Baldwin, from snooping on her own?

MISTLETOE MEDIUM, #3
Released: November 2015
ISBN: 9781310044779

No sooner does psychic Lottie Baldwin pull up stakes and move to Cheyenne, North Dakota, than she finds herself up to her neck in a series of mysterious robberies. Can Lottie and the handsome new man in her life, deputy sheriff Harlan Erikson, solve the crime spree before Lottie becomes the next victim?

OTHER BOOKS BY ELIZABETH

THE MIDNIGHT ZONE
Released: April 2013
ISBN: 9781301204182

When Cassie buys an antique compact, little does she know it can foretell the future—her future. Marjorie, a Florida girl unwillingly transplanted to Vermont, learns there's more to fear from the alien snowfall than just the cold. Neil Dallas's jagged descent from rock and roll singer to drug-addicted has-been is unstoppable . . . or is it?

Travel deep into unknown territory, where life and death are not as they seem; where you have to be careful what you ask for, because you might get it. These stories will take you beyond the realm of the solid and real, into the deepest, darkest corner of your imagination. Don't forget to bring your flashlight . . .

PRACTICAL PASSION
Released: April 2016
ISBN: 9781310079931

Julie Preston works hard raising her younger sister, Emily, giving up simple pleasures like love. When a friend drags her to a singles bar, Julie's meets Douglas and they spend several passionate hours together. When Julie hires a tutor for Emily, she's shocked to find Douglas from the bar. She has a hard time keeping her hands off him, but he isn't looking for a long-term relationship. Right?

SINCE ALL IS PASSING
Released: May 2016
ISBN: 9781310101458

When Marie Kenning witnesses the kidnapping of a child, she relives the horror of the death of her own family. Officer Chris Whitley takes on the case—and an interest in Marie—but evidence quickly indicates the child is dead. Marie discovers the kidnapper and his very-much-alive victim. Unable to convince Chris of the truth, she sets out alone on a dangerous cross-country mission to save the child.

A PORT IN THE STORM
Released: May 2016
ISBN: 9781310344824

Brian Nolan gave up his corporate job and moved home to Southingly, VT. He enjoys his job: plowing in winter and landscaping in summer. It doesn't pay much, but he has no interest in high-pressure work that comes with an ulcer and a broken relationship. Lately, He feels something lacking in his life, an unfulfilled need. Little does he know he'll find his reason for living stranded in a snowstorm.

www.ingramcontent.com/pod-product-compliance
Lightning Source LLC
Chambersburg PA
CBHW051240170626
46809CB00004B/1410